Charlotte Perkins Gilman's
"The Yellow Wall-paper"

THE PENN STATE SERIES IN THE HISTORY OF THE BOOK

James L. W. West III, General Editor

The series publishes books that employ a mixture of approaches: historical, archival, biographical, critical, sociological, and economic. Projected topics include professional authorship and the literary marketplace, the history of reading and book distribution, book-trade studies and publishing-house histories, and examinations of copyright and literary property.

Peter Burke, The Fortunes of the *Courtier*: The European Reception of Castiglione's *Cortegiano*

James M. Hutchisson, The Rise of Sinclair Lewis, 1920–1930

Julie Bates Dock, ed. Charlotte Perkins Gilman's "The Yellow Wall-paper" and the History of Its Publication and Reception: A Critical Edition and Documentary Casebook

John Williams, ed., Imaging the Early Medieval Bible

Penn State Reprints in Book History

James L. W. West III and Samuel S. Vaughan, Editors

Roger Burlingame, Of Making Many Books: A Hundred Years of Reading, Writing and Publishing

Julie Bates Dock

Compiler and Editor

Charlotte Perkins Gilman's "The Yellow Wall-paper" and the History of Its Publication and Reception

A Critical Edition and Documentary Casebook

The Pennsylvania State University Press
University Park, Pennsylvania

Library of Congress Cataloging-in-Publication Data

Gilman, Charlotte Perkins, 1860–1935.
  Charlotte Perkins Gilman's "The yellow wall-paper" and the History of Its Publication and
  Reception : a critical edition and documentary casebook / Julie Bates Dock, compiler and
  editor.
       p.   cm.—(The Penn State series in the history of the book)
  Includes bibliographical references.
  ISBN 0-271-01733-3 (cloth : alk. paper)
  ISBN 0-271-01734-1 (pbk. : alk. paper)
  1. Married women—Psychology—Fiction.   2. Mentally ill women—Fiction
  3. Sex role—Fiction.   4. Gilman, Charlotte Perkins, 1860–1935. Yellow wallpaper.
  5. Feminism and literature—United States.   6. Women and literature—
  United States.   7. Sex role in literature.   I. Dock, Julie Bates.   II. Title.
  III. Series.
  PS1744.G57Y45   1998
  813'.4—dc21   97-28775
                                                                              CIP

Introduction, critical edition of the text of "The Yellow Wall-paper," and textual notes and
apparatus Copyright © 1998 The Pennsylvania State University
All rights reserved
Printed in the United States of America
Published by The Pennsylvania State University Press,
University Park, PA 16802-1003

It is the policy of The Pennsylvania State University Press to use acid-free paper for the first
printing of all clothbound books. Publications on uncoated stock satisfy the minimum
requirements of American National Standard for Information Sciences—Permanence of
Paper for Printed Library Materials, ANSI Z39.48-1992.

Contents

Acknowledgments

My investigations into the story behind the story of "The Yellow Wall-paper" began with a simple collation exercise in an undergraduate course I offered on scholarly editing. I am grateful to the many students in that course who made preliminary collations of the story and who helped establish the relationships among various editions. Three of those students deserve special thanks and praise: Daphne Ryan Allen, Jennifer Palais, and Kristen Tracy worked with me for more than a year, tracking down reviews, comparing editions, and helping draft an article detailing our findings. Their insights and continued enthusiasm helped sustain the project to its first stage of completion. Portions of my introduction were first published in our collaborative article, "'But One Expects That': Charlotte Perkins Gilman's 'The Yellow Wallpaper' and the Shifting Light of Scholarship," *PMLA* 111 (January 1996), 52–65; they are reprinted by permission of the copyright owner, the Modern Language Association of America.

The community of Gilman scholars has been a source of support and stimulation throughout this project. I am particularly indebted to the pioneering scholarship and gracious encouragement of Gary Scharnhorst. Denise Knight and Shawn St. Jean offered valuable suggestions when some of my investigations had reached a dead end. Donald Ross and his students pointed me toward articles on S. Weir Mitchell's rest cure of which I was unaware.

This collection would not have been possible without the assistance of many librarians and archivists. My chief debt is to the dedicated staff of the Arthur and Elizabeth Schlesinger Library for the History of Women in America, especially Ellen Shea, Wendy Thomas, and Marie-Hélène Gold. My work at the Schlesinger was aided by a Radcliffe College Research Support Grant, for which I am most grateful. Steve Thacker of Loyola Marymount University kindly secured interlibrary loans that helped my work immeasurably. For archival assistance and permission to reprint items in their collections, I would also like to thank Charles Greifenstein, Tom Horrocks, and Kevin Crawford at the College of Physicians of Philadelphia; Martha King and Richard D. Stattler at the Rhode Island Historical Society; the Houghton Library of Harvard University; the Henry E. Huntington Memorial Library; the Boston Public Library; the Stowe-Day Center and Robinson Beecher Stowe.

Philip Winsor at Penn State Press encouraged my work long before I turned my attention to Gilman, and Sandy Thatcher supported this project from the outset. The comments and questions of James L. W. West III continually helped me refine and focus my arguments, and for his criticisms I am especially grateful.

My family and friends tirelessly cheered me on and I feel lucky to have had them by me always. Holli Levitsky, Susan Lesser, Phyllis Franzek, and Caroline Gebhard read early versions of my article and offered corrective suggestions with force and tact—I thank them for both. Charles sustained my spirit, Abigail sang away my cares, and Mom turned out to be a terrific research assistant.

★   ★   ★   ★   ★   ★

Finally, I dedicate this book to the next generation of Gilman scholars in the hope that it will stimulate their own research, lead them to question received legends, and cause them to be wary of their predecessors' conclusions—including mine.

Abbreviations

AMS   Autograph manuscript of "The Yellow Wall-paper," Charlotte Perkins Gilman Papers, Schlesinger Library, folder 221.

CI   *The Captive Imagination: A Casebook on "The Yellow Wallpaper."* Edited by Catherine Golden. New York: The Feminist Press at The City University of New York, 1992.

CPS   Charlotte Perkins Stetson (the name used between her marriage to Stetson in 1884 and her marriage to Gilman in 1900)

CPG   Charlotte Perkins Gilman (the name used after her marriage to Gilman in 1900)

CW   "The Yellow Wall-Paper." *American Mystery Stories.* Chosen by Carolyn Wells. N.p.: Oxford University Press, American Branch, 1927. Pp. 176–97.

Diaries   *The Diaries of Charlotte Perkins Gilman.* Edited by Denise D. Knight. 2 vols. Charlottesville: University Press of Virginia, 1994.

FP   *The Yellow Wallpaper.* Edited with an Afterword by Elaine R. Hedges. New York: The Feminist Press at The City University of New York, 1973.

FP2   *The Yellow Wall-Paper.* Edited with an Afterword by Elaine R. Hedges. Revised Edition: A Complete and Accurate Rendition of the 1892 Edition, with a New Note on the Text. New York: The Feminist Press at The City University of New York, 1996.

GB   "The Yellow Wall-Paper." *The Golden Book Magazine* 18 (October 1933), 363–73.

GR   "The Yellow Wallpaper." *The Charlotte Perkins Gilman Reader: "The Yellow Wallpaper" and Other Fiction.* Edited and introduced by Ann J. Lane. New York: Pantheon Books, 1980. Pp. 3–19.

Journey *A Journey from Within: The Love Letters of Charlotte Perkins Gilman, 1897–1900*. Edited and annotated by Mary A. Hill. Lewisburg, PA.: Bucknell University Press, 1995.

Living *The Living of Charlotte Perkins Gilman: An Autobiography*. New York: Appleton-Century, 1935.

NE "The Yellow Wall-paper." *The New England Magazine*, n.s. 5 (January 1892), 647–56.

SM *The Yellow Wall Paper*. Boston: Small, Maynard & Co., 1899.

WDH "The Yellow Wall Paper." *The Great Modern American Stories: An Anthology*. Compiled and edited with an introduction by William Dean Howells. New York: Boni and Liveright, 1920. Pp. 320–37.

WW *The Yellow Wallpaper*. Edited and with an introduction by Thomas L. Erskine and Connie L. Richards. Women Writers: Texts and Contexts Series. New Brunswick, N.J.: Rutgers University Press, 1993. Pp. 29–50.

The Legend of
"The Yellow Wall-paper"

In the two decades since the Feminist Press issued its slim volume containing a text of "The Yellow Wall-paper" with an afterword by Elaine R. Hedges, Charlotte Perkins Gilman's remarkable work has been as completely canonized as any work of literature can claim to be. Hedges's edition has sold more than 225,000 copies, becoming the Feminist Press's "all-time best-seller."[1] Omitting "The Yellow Wall-paper" from an American literature anthology has become almost as unthinkable as leaving out "The Raven" or "Civil Disobedience." The story appears not just in hefty, two-volume collections of American literature, but in textbooks for women's studies and genre studies courses, and more especially in the dozens of introductory literature texts that undergraduates purchase by the gross. Numerous editions offer the story to readers around the globe: in Gilman's own lifetime it was translated into Finnish, and just recently a Hebrew translation was published.[2] "The Yellow Wall-paper" has been celebrated and analyzed by literary historians of every stripe, though feminist critics still lead the way in championing Gilman's achievement.

Gilman's masterpiece has a well-established and well-deserved place in the canon of world literature. In its twenty-five-year odyssey of rediscovery by literary critics, however, the story has picked up along the way an assortment of blemishes and distortions, from textual anomalies to skewed accounts of its publication history to misinformation about its contemporary reception. A survey of these textual and interpretive problems will make clear the need for the present volume, which offers the first critical edition of "The Yellow Wall-paper" along with a selection of

---

1. The Feminist Press at CUNY, 1995 Catalog, p. 29.
2. "Keltainen Seinapaperi," trans. Irene Tokoi, *Nykyaika*, 15 June 1934, 1–7; "Neyar ha-kir ha-tsahov," trans. E. Morag (Hod ha-Sharon: Astrolog, 1995).

documents relevant to its publication and reception histories. But first, a word about the role of primary materials in literary interpretation.

In her useful introduction to an issue of *PMLA* devoted to the status of evidence, Heather Dubrow writes, "In the discipline of literary studies, even though one should not posit a lost Eden of naive but joyous positivism, the distrust of evidence and of those who adduce it has surely intensified in the past two or three decades."[3] In many quarters, the notion of objective or empirical evidence has been routinely pooh-poohed, and practitioners of traditional modes of criticism—such as textual scholarship—have been dismissed as simplistic in their faith in documentary evidence. Though detractors of traditional evidentiary procedures and materials sometimes overzealously attribute to earlier critics what Dubrow calls "an unthinking confidence about proof" ("Status," p. 11), they have nonetheless raised awareness of how the scholar participates in the process of constructing, and not just unearthing, evidence, and they have called attention to the consequent difficulty (if not the impossibility) of reading evidence without bias. Yet the same poststructuralists who deprecate the value of evidence can find themselves hoist with their own petard: their ingenious interpretations of unstable texts often rely on texts whose instability has been exacerbated by their own disregard for textual evidence. A middle ground between the extremes of naive positivism and naive skepticism would, perhaps, be a firmer place to stand. Just as we should not implicitly believe that documents have an unambiguous or final say in our reconstructions of past events, we need not cavalierly reject the validity of documentary evidence.

This problem can be compounded by the inaccessibility of the documents themselves. How much easier it is to dismiss documentary evidence when such evidence is unavailable or inconveniently located, when it has to be pried out of manuscript archives and back issues of long-forgotten newspapers. The letters reprinted in this volume, to give a fairly straightforward example, are culled from four collections at three institutions, and the reviews come from more than twenty magazines and newspapers, many of them obscure publications archived only in their immediate place of publication, if at all. This problem has certainly afflicted scholarship on Gilman's "The Yellow Wall-paper," and perhaps on other of her works as well.

Elsewhere I have argued that the use of documents is affected by critical trends and by critics' biases and expectations.[4] Criticism of "The Yellow Wall-paper" in the past quarter-century shows the effects of this dynamic. Feminist critics of the early 1970s, intent on establishing women authors in the American literary canon, had a stake in portraying the story as a victimized piece of literature. The notion that

---

3. "The Status of Evidence," *PMLA* 111 (January 1996), 12.
4. Julie Bates Dock, with Daphne Ryan Allen, Jennifer Palais, and Kristen Tracy, " 'But One Expects That': Charlotte Perkins Gilman's 'The Yellow Wallpaper' and the Shifting Light of Scholarship," *PMLA* 111 (January 1996), 52–65.

Gilman suffered condemnation from editors and readers outside the story tidily echoed the narrator's victimization within the story. When critics found powerful statements in Gilman's memoirs that confirmed their expectations of a hostile male response to the story, they often looked no further for corroboration or contradiction of the author's assertions. Scholars of the 1980s and 1990s built their own interpretations on this shaky foundation, repeating and embellishing the publication and reception histories of "The Yellow Wall-paper" until the whole edifice has come to look like a shrine to beleaguered women authors everywhere (including women critics within academe). Any challenge to the Gilman hagiography, therefore, implicitly challenges a school of feminist thought that views the publishing world, the literary canon, and, by extension, academe as exclusively patriarchal domains.[5]

The present collection brings together materials relevant to the story's publication and reception, along with documents that shed light on Gilman's attitudes toward authorship. These materials do not explicitly support or refute any single interpretation of the story or its history. Instead, they are intended to allow new readers of "The Yellow Wall-paper" to draw their own conclusions about the textual and reception histories of the story, and to stimulate Gilman scholars to question their assumptions about the story and the facts surrounding it. I hope this edition and collection will let readers focus on Gilman's masterly indictment of the treatment endured by the narrator of her story rather than on any treatment Gilman endured as an author. Even more, I hope it will allow the next wave of scholars to ask new questions about "The Yellow Wall-paper" and the impact it has had on readers for more than a hundred years.

"In my judgment," wrote Gilman in her autobiography, "it is a pretty poor thing to write . . . without a purpose" (page 89). As I believe many of the reviews and letters included here demonstrate, her autobiographical statements can and should be regarded as stories with a purpose, texts crafted to create particular impressions in the minds of her audience. Similarly, the present selection of documents necessarily reflects the editor's own interests (some would say biases), as do the annotations and critical framing of those items. Readers should approach all these materials as critically as they would Gilman's fiction if they would steer clear of the twin shoals of unexamined positivism and knee-jerk skepticism.

5. Responses to my article demonstrate how personally identified some critics seem to be with the prevailing views of Gilman's story. See Scott Heller, "How a Writer Became a Feminist Legend," *Chronicle of Higher Education* (19 January 1996), A10, and the letter from Elaine Hedges and Catherine Golden in the Forum section of *PMLA* 111 (May 1996), 467–68.

A BRIEF HISTORY OF EDITIONS

On June 6 and 7, 1890, Charlotte Stetson sat in her Southern California cottage and wrote the story for which she is best known today. "The Yellow Wall-paper" was written, according to her note on its history, "in two days, with the thermometer at one hundred and three—in Pasadena, Cal." The region had experienced an unusually wet and chilly spring, but in early June the weather warmed up substantially— and briefly. After two days in the nineties, the Los Angeles *Times* records a high of 102 degrees on June 6, with the following day soaring to 105 before the temperature returned to the mid-seventies. One week later Gilman reports sending "The Yellow Wall-paper" to *Scribner's*—the first mention of the story that survives in her papers. Eighteen months elapsed before her tale saw print for the first time, but since then it has been reissued at least once in every decade.

The New England Magazine first published "The Yellow Wallpaper" in January 1892. Small, Maynard & Co., the publishers of Gilman's *Women and Economics* (1898) and *In This Our World* (1898), issued the story as a monograph in June 1899, reissuing the same edition in 1901 and 1911. With the author's permission, the story was anthologized by William Dean Howells in *The Great Modern American Stories* (1920), by Carolyn Wells in *American Mystery Stories* (1927), and by E. A. Cross in *A Book of the Short Story* (1934). Gilman also authorized reprintings in the *New York Evening Post* (1922) and *The Golden Book Magazine* (1933). Printed at least seven times before Gilman's death in 1935, the story appeared regularly in anthologies for the next four decades, though modern critics would have it otherwise.

"For almost fifty years," lament Sandra M. Gilbert and Susan Gubar, "*The Yellow Wallpaper* went unprinted and unread." Similarly, Annette Kolodny attributes the story's lack of influence on later women authors to its being "so quickly relegated to the backwaters of our literary landscape."[6] The print record belies these claims. Between Gilman's death and the Feminist Press edition of 1973, the story was anthologized in 1937, 1938, 1941, 1942, 1943, 1948, 1950, 1961, 1965, 1966, 1967, 1971, and three times in 1972 (see Appendix: Printings of "The Yellow Wall-paper," pages 121–32). "The Yellow Wall-paper" joined collections of works by women authors, it accompanied tales of the macabre and chilling horror, it sat alongside psychological thrillers. It was published in mass-market paperbacks, in illustrated hardbound editions, and in college textbooks. Having seen print nearly two dozen times since 1892, the story was by no means unavailable to readers in the first three-quarters of the twentieth century, though it may be argued that it reached the common reader far more readily than the scholar.

6. Gilbert and Gubar, eds., *The Norton Anthology of Literature by Women: The Tradition in English* (New York: Norton, 1985), p. 1148. Kolodny, "A Map for Rereading; or, Gender and the Interpretation of Literary Texts," *New Literary History* 11 (1980), 459.

Charlotte Perkins Stetson

1894.

Fig. 1. Charlotte Perkins Stetson, c. 1890. Though dated "1894" on the front, the photo is labeled on the back "Taken in Pasadena, age of 30" with the date of 1890 added in Katherine Stetson Chamberlin's hand, along with the note: "This is—we all thought—excellent—KSC". In her diary Gilman records a visit to a photographer on 6 October 1890; she picked up the photo on the 11th and remarked that it was "*Splendid*" (*Diaries*, p. 421). Reprinted by permission of the Schlesinger Library, Radcliffe College.

Elaine Hedges's edition of 1973 gave "The Yellow Wall-paper" wider academic readership than ever before. Hedges's text was immediately anthologized in count-less college textbooks, and it can justly claim to be the starting point for the literary establishment's renewed interest in Gilman and her work. But what was that text? The copyright page claims the edition is a "Reprint of the 1899 ed. published by Small, Maynard, Boston." Collation of the text, however, shows that it instead reprints the 1892 *New England Magazine* text, throwing in a few variants of its own. Some are typos with little significance—for instance, "phospsites" for "phosphites" (page 29, line 23; all citations of the story shall be to the present edition by page and line number) but toward the end of the story there is an omission of two sentences.

Hedges's edition prompted so much interest in Gilman that in 1980 Ann Lane edited *The Charlotte Perkins Gilman Reader*, an anthology that made available more of Gilman's work to a wide and eager audience. A source note implies that Lane's reprinting of "The Yellow Wall-paper" derives from the 1892 *New England Maga-zine* version. Instead it republishes a text based on the 1933 reprint in the popular *Golden Book Magazine*, a version that contains many anomalies of wording and section breaks. While Hedges's edition was erroneously labeled a reprint of the 1899 edition, Lane's was incorrectly billed as the 1892 text when it was copied into numerous college anthologies.

The 1992 centennial of the story prompted the publication of Catherine Golden's *The Captive Imagination: A Casebook on "The Yellow Wallpaper,"* which the Feminist Press markets as a "critical edition," a phrase Golden repeats in her introduction (*CI*, p. 19). According to a footnote, the edition reprints the 1899 text along with the illustrations from the 1892 magazine, reprinted now for the first time.[7] A close look at the text easily confirms that Golden and the Feminist Press have simply reissued Hedges's 1973 text. Even the typos have been preserved. Moreover, the omitted lines are restored in a footnote that rings with the scholarly authority customarily accorded to critical editions: Golden introduces the lines by saying, "Here, the 1892 edition of 'The Yellow Wallpaper' includes the following passage" (*CI*, p. 38). She misleadingly informs readers that the 1899 edition omits the lines, while the 1892 edition includes them, when no such variant exists between the two texts. The only text to omit those lines was Hedges's 1973 reissue of the 1892 text, erroneously billed as a reprint of 1899.

The editors of the story in the Rutgers University Press series "Women Writers: Texts and Contexts," Thomas L. Erskine and Connie L. Richards, claim their "authoritative" text is "From *New England Magazine*, January 1892" (p. 29), and to a large extent it is. Unfortunately, that is not the whole story. Aware of the

---

7. The final illustration showing the narrator crawling over her prostrate husband has been reversed in its reproduction in the volume. The Feminist Press has said it will correct the illustration if *The Captive Imagination* goes into a second printing.

discrepancies between Hedges's and Lane's texts, these editors seem to have tried to split the difference between the two. When variants arise, they choose now from one text, now from the other, giving no rationale for their choices. They restore the lines missing from Hedges's text but also include words added in the 1933 text Lane reprinted. What Erskine and Richards have created, then, is a text that never was on sea or land, a text that includes the *most* words, if not necessarily the *right* words.

In an age when the very hyphen in "wall-paper" receives its share of critical ink as a "signifier,"[8] even a minor textual variant has potential consequences for literary interpretation. The confused array of texts that has appeared in the past two decades presents dozens of small but potentially significant variants. Indeed, some of the variants that have crept into "The Yellow Wall-paper" are far from minor, especially those that bear on gender issues in the story. Two examples will help to make this clear.

The first important variant, and the one most noticeably resonant with meaning, appears in the fifth paragraph of the story. After declaring that there is "something queer" about the house they have rented, the narrator remarks, "John laughs at me, of course, but one expects that in marriage" (29.9). Texts that follow *The Golden Book Magazine* (and Lane's more recent *Gilman Reader*) print the following: "John laughs at me, of course, but one expects that." Omitting "in marriage" radically transforms the line. Why on earth would one "expect that"? Does John laugh at her because she is genuinely funny? because he thinks her a silly little woman? because she feels the house is creepy? because John is a jerk? We cannot know. Clearly other readers do not know either, for several have attempted to clarify this ambiguity. In addition to the truncated "expects that" version, editors have added loaded meanings such as "one expects that in [him]," "one expects that in John," "one expects that in men," and "one expects that in man."[9] These readings either personalize the statement specifically to John or universalize it to include all men. In the first case, readers may conclude that John laughs at the narrator for reasons relating to his own character. In the second, the narrator engages in obvious male-bashing, which, though perhaps amusing, sets a definite tone for the rest of the story. More important, it distorts Gilman's focus; here she is bashing marriage in particular, not men in general.

At the close of the story there is another intriguing variant. After John pounds

---

8. See Richard Feldstein, "Reader, Text, and Ambiguous Referentiality in 'The Yellow Wall-Paper,'" in Golden, *CI*, pp. 307–18.

9. Gail Parker, ed., *The Oven Birds: American Women on Womanhood, 1820–1920* (Garden City, N.Y.: Doubleday, 1972), p. 317; Joan Kahn, ed., *Open at Your Own Risk* (Boston: Houghton Mifflin, 1975), p. 1; CW, p. 177; Joyce Carol Oates, ed., *The Oxford Book of American Short Stories* (Oxford: Oxford University Press, 1992), p. 154.

ineffectually at the narrator's locked door, she reports, "Now he's crying for an axe" (42.8). Textual descendants of *The Golden Book* render the line "Now he's crying to Jennie for an axe."[10] The original wording allows readers to imagine a powerless John calling—even crying—for assistance, thereby undermining his masculinity and showing his wife gaining the upper hand, at least emotionally. The variant reading, "crying to Jennie for an axe," reempowers John, placing him in a dominant position vis-à-vis another woman, this time Jennie: he demands an axe and cries out because the seriousness of the situation requires Jennie to obey quickly. By saying he is crying *to Jennie*, another twist is added: Jennie becomes John's overt accomplice in repressing the narrator. While this might be a valid interpretation (other evidence in the story suggests that Jennie acts as jailer in John's absence), it is not what Gilman stressed in this line.

Other substantive variants have similar consequences for critical interpretation. Compare, for instance, the reading in the first printing, "He said we came here solely on my account" with the later reading, "He said he came here solely on my account" (30.33). Or, after John carries the narrator upstairs to comfort her, the magazine version records that he read to her until "it tired my head" while the book version reads "he tired my head" (35.15). Likewise, John admonishes her not to "let any silly fancies run away with me," but those become "my silly fancies" (35.19) in 1899.

Another class of variants concerns section breaks, often considered among the accidentals of a text, but substantive in the case of "The Yellow Wall-paper." The story is presented as if it were the narrator's private journal, with the section breaks demarcating her putative diary entries.[11] Gilman uses these breaks to depict the narrator's circumstances as well as her mental state. She must break off writing in her secret journal each time she hears her husband or sister-in-law draw near. The interruptions are signaled by such phrases as "There comes John, and I must put this away—he hates to have me write a word" (31.14), or "There's sister on the stairs!" (33.26). These disruptions put the narrator at the mercy of those who wish to suppress her writing.

If critics are right in thinking that the section breaks correspond to diary entries and have some interpretive value (Haney-Peritz even refers to them as "movements" [*CI*, p. 266]), then editors owe it to critics to preserve all the breaks that

---

10. Evidence points to GB as the source for the reading. There the variant reads "to Jenny", though John's sister's name is consistently spelled "Jennie" elsewhere in the story. All other versions regularize the spelling as "Jennie" in this line.

11. Several critics have explored the contradictions inherent in this form. See, for instance, Paula A. Treichler, "Escaping the Sentence: Diagnosis and Discourse in 'The Yellow Wallpaper,'" in Golden, *CI*, pp. 191–210, and Janice Haney-Peritz, "Monumental Feminism and Literature's Ancestral House: Another Look at 'The Yellow Wallpaper,'" in Golden, *CI*, pp. 261–76.

Gilman herself authorized, and only those breaks. The breaks Gilman indicates in a surviving manuscript match those reproduced in the first printing and in three of the other reprintings during Gilman's lifetime. The pattern of section breaks begins to change dramatically in 1933 when *The Golden Book* adds five new breaks and omits seven of the original ones. Elimination of section breaks associates phrases that were not presented together before and alters the character of the narrator. For instance, all prior texts had inserted a break between the two sentences "I will take a nap, I guess" and "I don't know why I should write this" (34.35–37). *The Golden Book* deletes this break, situating the two sentences during the same writing session and making the narrator appear indecisive. Until this point, readers might see her as emotional and fanciful, but never ambivalent—she is constant in her need to discover the wallpaper's secrets. The added breaks also affect interpretation. One such break is inserted between John's question, "Can you not trust me as a physician when I tell you so?" and the narrator's internal response, "So of course I said no more on that score, and we went to sleep before long" (36.33–34). Another added break disrupts the narrator's speculations about whether the woman behind the wallpaper gets out in the daytime: "I can see her out of every one of my windows!" now ends one section, while the next section begins "It is the same woman, I know" (39.30–31). A break between such closely related sentences makes little sense, unless it is meant to show eccentric behavior in the narrator, who seems to be pausing between journal entries before she completes a thought. But earlier versions of the story demonstrate that the narrator *can* complete her thoughts unless she is interrupted and forced to stop writing.

The number of section breaks is as vexed a question as the placement of those breaks. Gilman's manuscript and three early printings divide "The Yellow Wallpaper" into twelve sections, while *The Golden Book* and Cross use only ten sections. Subsequent texts have offered readers fewer and fewer diary entries, though the overall length of the story remains constant. Texts based on the Small, Maynard edition often omit one or more of the section breaks at 37.4, 39.14, and 40.11, for these fall at the end of a full page and are easily overlooked. Texts based on the 1973 Feminist Press edition encounter similar problems. Hedges's edition preserves Gilman's original sections, but instead of signaling the beginning of each new section typographically (with asterisks, an enlarged capital, or a combination of large and small capitals, as in earlier editions), the Feminist Press simply uses a blank line to separate sections. Gilman's breaks at 34.36 and 35.35 fall at page breaks (*FP*, pp. 20–21 and 22–23), and the blank line goes unnoticed in many editions based on this text. Thus Catherine Golden can explain that "the story is comprised of ten diary-like entries" (*CI*, p. 12), for by the time she transmits the text those two end-of-page section breaks have disappeared. Moreover, texts based on Golden's edition will likely reduce the story to nine "diary-like entries" for the same reason:

the break after the narrator's remark that "There is a week more, and I think that will be enough" (38.19) falls at the bottom of a page and before an illustration in her edition; later editors might well miss it.[12] Ann Lane's *Gilman Reader* modifies the eccentric tradition begun by *The Golden Book* and produces a story with seven sections. Most recently, Erskine and Richards's "authoritative text" picks and chooses between the two traditions of section breaks in modern editions, presenting a story composed of only six sections.

"The Yellow Wall-paper" deserves a thorough textual analysis to clarify the discrepancies among the varying editions and reduce gratuitous textual instability. This volume presents a critical edition of the story based on collation of all relevant texts. A textual introduction chronicles the story's publication history, describes Gilman's attitudes toward publication and authorship, and explains the editorial methodology and the rationale for the copy-text of the present edition, the 1892 *New England Magazine* version of the story. Following the clear reading text of "The Yellow Wall-paper" are three tables that enable the reader to reconstruct the changes the story has undergone. The list of Editorial Emendations (pages 70–71) records the present edition's alterations of the copy-text, while the list of Pre-copy-text Substantive Variants (pages 71–74) presents all the discrepancies that exist between Gilman's surviving manuscript and the first printing. The Historical Collation (pages 74–80) records the variants introduced by the important editions subsequent to the story's initial publication, including every relevant text from 1899 until 1994. Additionally, an Appendix: Printings of "The Yellow Wall-paper" (pages 121–32) records all reprintings discovered for the years prior to 1973, and a representative selection of subsequent appearances of the story in anthologies, noting the textual source of each reprinting.

PUBLICATION LEGENDS

Since the renaissance in Gilman studies began in 1973, scholars have accumulated a wealth of information about her life in general and "The Yellow Wall-paper" in particular. Some facts about the story's publication and reception have become common knowledge in the natural process that occurs as critics build on and reiterate

12. Since these problems were noted in my article, the Feminist Press has issued a revised edition of *The Yellow Wall-Paper* in which the section breaks are clearly signaled by a row of spaced asterisks. The press has also announced plans to clarify the section breaks in a second printing of Golden's *Captive Imagination* (date unknown).

each other's work. Gilman's valiant struggle to get her story into print, the original audience's reading of it as a ghost story, the irate reception it received from the male medical community—these are some of the legends that have adhered to "The Yellow Wall-paper" and have gone unchallenged for more than twenty years. However, many of these "facts" upon which interpretations have been built don't hold up well under scrutiny.

Scholars who have told the publication history of "The Yellow Wall-paper" have had to wrestle with two well-known versions of that history, Gilman's and W. D. Howells's. By now, a standard interpretation of the divergent accounts has been accepted, not least because it has been so often repeated. Everyone agrees that Gilman first sent the story to the noted editor Howells, who had praised her earlier work. On receiving the unsolicited story in early October 1890, Howells sent it to Horace Elisha Scudder, then editor of the *Atlantic Monthly*, with a note telling Scudder, "It's pretty blood curdling, but strong, and is certainly worth reading" (page 91). Scudder rejected it, saying, according to Howells's account, "that it was too terribly good to be printed" (page 118). In her autobiography, Gilman recalls Scudder telling her that the story made him "miserable." At this point, accounts of the story's fate differ fundamentally. Gilman claims in *The Living* that she then gave the manuscript to Henry Austin, a commercial literary agent who eventually placed the story with *The New England Magazine*. She reprints her peevish letter to the magazine's editor, demanding to know if he pays his contributors. Her indignation reaches its apex when she relates that Austin apparently pocketed her profits from the publication (page 87). In contrast, Howells recalls that after learning of Scudder's rejection, he "could not rest until [he] had corrupted the editor of *The New England Magazine* into publishing it" (pages 117–18).

Faced with these conflicting accounts, most of the recent critics have sided with Gilman in her dismissal of Howells, as evidenced by Catherine Golden's centennial collection of critical essays. Of the critics in *The Captive Imagination* who discuss Howells's role in the story's publication, three ignore his claim altogether. Others take Gilman's account at face value, in spite of its inaccurate dates and titles. Earliest and most strident, Gail Parker chides Howells in 1972 for his "misgivings" about the story and claims he "was really the enemy" of American feminists (*CI*, pp. 85, 89). Hedges offers more measured criticism of Howells, saying that his "admiration for the story . . . limited itself to the story's 'chilling' quality" (*CI*, p. 41). Gradually, critics begin to cast Gilman in a heroic mold, telling us, as Conrad Shumaker did in 1985, that after Scudder's rejection "Gilman persevered" and got the story published (*CI*, p. 242). Golden scolds Howells for what she calls his "self-congratulatory tone" and his "belief" that he had something to do with the story's acceptance (*CI*, p. 55).

The most recent collection of essays on "The Yellow Wall-paper" proposes a handy compromise between Howells's version and Gilman's: Erskine and Richards maintain that "Gilman hired Henry Austin, a literary agent, who finally placed the story, with Howells's intervention and support, in *New England Magazine* in 1892" (WW, p. 7). The notion that Austin and Howells somehow acted in concert appears unlikely given the unfriendly terms of their relationship. Just a few months before this supposed collaboration, Austin had sent Howells a copy of his recent book, *Vagabond Verses*, hoping, he said, only for "some courteous note of acknowledgement." Instead, Howells reviewed the volume of poetry in the May 1891 issue of *Harper's*, prompting Austin to write a long and scathing letter to the man he regarded as his enemy. He objects that, "in a magazine of great circulation and influence where, of course, no friend of mine has a chance to defend me, [Howells] seized the occasion to kick me for my courtesy." Austin goes on to accuse Howells of literary snobbery and bad breeding, concluding that "I have long known that you do not like me personally."[13] In light of this animosity, the likelihood of their cooperation on Gilman's behalf seems scant.

How, then, should we resolve the he-says/she-says conundrum? What evidence exists to support Gilman's or Howells's versions of events?

Gilman's manuscript log and diary substantiate her sending the manuscript to Austin after Scudder's rejection of it. Yet there is no clear link between the agent and the story's publication. When Gilman sent her poem "Similar Cases" to *The Nationalist* in March 1890, Henry Willard Austin was listed on its masthead as the journal's editor. Gilman's poem, published in the April 1890 number, earned high praise and was reprinted the following September in *The New England Magazine*, edited by Edwin Doak Mead. Such reprintings were common enough during this period, and need not have occasioned any contact between Mead and either Austin or his successor, Edward Bellamy, who took over the editorship during the summer. The two journals shared many of the same interests and contributors. Chief among them was Gilman's uncle by marriage, Edward Everett Hale, who wrote for *The Nationalist* and was listed as an editor of *The New England Magazine* from its founding in September 1889 until November 1890. Hale seems to have served as Gilman's pipeline to publication in *The New England Magazine* at least once: Gilman sent him "An Anti-Nationalist Wail" on 16 September 1890, a week before she first heard from Henry Austin, and the poem appeared in the December number under the title "For Sweet Charity's Sake."

When Gilman received a letter from Austin on 23 September 1890, literary agents were only just beginning to appear on the American publishing scene, though they were already active in England. The connection between author and agent was usually informal and would not be clearly delineated until after the turn of the

13. Henry Austin to W. D. Howells, [May 1891], 6 pp., Houghton Autograph File, Houghton Library, Harvard University. Quoted by permission.

Fig. 2. W. D. Howells, 1896. Photo by L. Alman & Co., 172 Fifth Ave., N.Y. & Newport, R.I. Reprinted by permission of the Houghton Library, Harvard University.

century.[14] In 1890, Austin was no longer editor of *The Nationalist* and was instead acting on behalf of "Traveller Literary Syndicate," an organization that apparently

14. Little has been written about the activities of literary agents in the United States before 1900. The best general account remains Donald Sheehan's *This Was Publishing: A Chronicle of the Book Trade in the Gilded Age* (Bloomington: Indiana University Press, 1952). James Harper, *The Author's Empty Purse and the Rise of the Literary Agent* (London: Oxford University Press, 1968), gives a good account of agents in England and contains a brief chapter on "Agency in America: Newspaper Agencies, Societies for Authors, Marbury and Reynolds" (pp. 67–75).

Fig. 3. Horace E. Scudder, no date. Reprinted by permission of the Houghton Library, Harvard University.

also involved Hale. Gilman sent Austin eleven poems four days after receiving his letter; she forwarded "The Yellow Wall-paper" the following month, the same day that she sent ten "Mer-Songs" to "Uncle Edward (Traveller Literary Syndicate)."[15] Some of the eleven poems Gilman sent to Austin were eventually published, but they were published in magazines to which Gilman herself submitted them between

15. I have located no other link between Hale and Traveller Literary Syndicate.

November 1890 and January 1891. Austin seems to have had no hand in placing the poems, and Gilman never mentions any agreement with an agent or Traveller Literary Syndicate. Indeed, after the brief diary notation in February 1891 that "Mr. Henry Austin sent me his book—'Vagabond Verses,'" he seems to vanish from Gilman's life until she excoriates him forty years later for absconding with the payment for "The Yellow Wall-paper." Perhaps Austin told the truth when he "denied having got the money," as Gilman relates in *The Living*; he might have received no payment because he had no role in the story's publication, despite Gilman's oft-repeated tale of being swindled.

And what of Howells's version of events? If Howells scholars are correct in characterizing him as an honest and modest autobiographer,[16] it would seem unlikely that he invented the episode or exaggerated his own contribution to the story's publication. Regardless of his track record, the very existence of his claim to have "corrupted" an editor provides ample reason for scholars to investigate. In fact, that corrupted editor was the first cousin of Howells's wife Elinor. Edwin Mead was more than kin; he had himself benefited from Howells's patronage. Just when Howells had become influential as the assistant editor of *The Atlantic Monthly*, he brought the seventeen-year-old Mead to Boston from New Hampshire and got him a job with Ticknor and Fields, the famous Boston publishing house. Recalling his early years in Boston, Mead wrote: "The doors to the larger Boston life were opened to me by William Dean Howells, to whom my debt of gratitude for service then and growing service and inspiration ever afterwards is very great."[17] Elsewhere in the same memoir Mead remarks that "To the end of his life Howells was pre-eminently my 'guide, philosopher and friend,' and, as the days go on, he bulks ever larger in my mind" (p. 30). It would seem that Howells could easily have influenced his wife's grateful cousin. Had he used that gratitude for his own ends, he might well have been reluctant to elaborate publicly on his machinations, which could account for his coy reference nearly three decades later to a form of corruption. Either Gilman did not know or she forgot about Howells's claim to have a hand in the story's eventual publication when she penned her memoirs. According to Joanne B. Karpinski's study of Gilman's relationship with Howells, her "failure to credit Howells . . . follow[ed] a pattern of denying the actual contributions of those who, in Gilman's opinion, ought to have done more."[18]

16. On Howells's "high standard of honesty" in his memoirs, see, for example, Kenneth Lynn, *William Dean Howells: An American Life* (New York: Harcourt, Brace, 1970), pp. 39–40, 320; and Edwin H. Cady, *The Realist at War: The Mature Years, 1885–1920, of William Dean Howells* (Syracuse: Syracuse University Press, 1958), pp. 204–8.

17. "Boston Memories of Fifty Years," *Fifty Years of Boston: A Memorial Volume*, ed. Elisabeth M. Herlihy (Boston: Subcommittee on Memorial History of the Boston Tercentenary Committee, 1932), p. 8.

18. "When the Marriage of True Minds Admits Impediments: Charlotte Perkins Gilman and William

In any case, the story of a heroic woman author fighting valiantly in defiance of a thwarting male editorial presence makes for great drama, capped as it is with the male agent's theft of the profit that should have gone to the woman who would later write *Women and Economics*. Elizabeth Ammons comments, quite accurately though without any apparent irony, that this outcome "seems almost unbelievably fitting."[19] Perhaps things that are unbelievable should *not* be believed—at least not without corroborating evidence.

RECEPTION LEGENDS

If the story's publication history has become part of the Gilman hagiography, entrenched ideas about its initial reception—as a ghost story or as a story that angry male doctors sought to suppress—contribute even more to the mythology surrounding Gilman. When Elaine Hedges reintroduced "The Yellow Wall-paper" to the literary world, she remarked in her Afterword that "in its time . . . the story was read essentially as a Poe-esque tale of chilling horror—and as a story of mental aberration" (FP, p. 39). Gilman herself made the analogy with Poe, first in a private letter to Martha Luther Lane and later in the public forum of her autobiography (see pages 90 and 87). The chilling qualities of the tale certainly drew the attention of its early readers: writing in *The Conservator* in 1899, Anne Montgomerie praises the story for its "perfect crescendo of horror," while an anonymous Baltimore reviewer notes that the piece "has a touch of ghastliness" (pages 104 and 106). Similarly, in the introduction to his anthology, Howells points to the story's ability to "freeze our young blood" and remarks that "I shiver over it as much as I did when I first read it in manuscript" (pages 117–18). The horror of aberrant behavior or extreme psychological pressure unquestionably captured the attention of the early readers of "The Yellow Wall-paper," but there is a definite distinction between a tale of horrors and a tale of ghosts.

Feminist critics after Hedges blurred this distinction and suggested that the story's early readers embraced a supernatural interpretation of the story. Ann Lane introduces the ghostly element into the story's reception history when she asserts that "horror writer H. P. Lovecraft called ['The Yellow Wall-paper'] one of the great 'spectral tales' in American literature" (*Gilman Reader*, p. xvii). Unfortunately, no source for Lovecraft's putative remark is cited. Catherine Golden follows up on

---

Dean Howells," *Patrons and Protégées: Gender, Friendship, and Writing in Nineteenth-Century America*, ed. Shirley Marchalonis (New Brunswick: Rutgers University Press, 1988), p. 228.

19. *Conflicting Stories: American Women Writers at the Turn into the Twentieth Century* (New York: Oxford University Press, 1991), p. 42.

Lane's tantalizing lead in *The Captive Imagination*. She supports the ghost-story claim when she states, "As recently as 1973, horror writer H. P. Lovecraft included ['The Yellow Wall-paper'] as a 'classic example in subtly delineating the madness which crawls over a woman dwelling in the hideously papered room' in a collection titled *Supernatural Horror in Literature*" (*CI*, p. 3). If we turn to Lovecraft to find Gilman's story interpreted and anthologized as a supernatural tale, we are once again disappointed. Although Golden characterizes Lovecraft's book as a "collection" of supernatural tales, it is actually a critical study of the whole spectrum of horror tales in world literature. He mentions Gilman only in passing, praising the writer herself for "ris[ing] to a classic level" in her delineation of madness.[20] Golden's support for the ghost-story reading relies on a mischaracterization of Lovecraft's volume. Then too, the recentness of Lovecraft's work is suspect. The copyright page indicates that the 1973 edition is a reprint of a 1945 collection of essays. Moreover, Golden implies that Lovecraft played an active part in the 1973 collection; since he died in 1937 this is probably not the case (though with a writer of the supernatural, one is never sure).

Ever since Lane noted that "'The Yellow Wallpaper' has often been reprinted as a horror story," modern critics have assumed that early anthologists valued Gilman's masterpiece only for its chilling qualities and grouped it with other tales in the Poe tradition. Lane points to Howells's 1920 anthology as the story's "most famous appearance in that genre" (*Gilman Reader*, p. xvii). However, Howells's *Great Modern American Stories* can be regarded as a collection of horror stories only if the definition of the term "horror" is stretched to include Twain's "Celebrated Jumping Frog," Harte's "Outcasts of Poker Flat," or Freeman's "The Revolt of 'Mother.'" Lane's assertion would seem to be better supported by other anthologies, such as Carolyn Wells's *American Mystery Stories* (1927) or Philip Van Doren Stern's *Midnight Reader: Great Stories of Haunting and Horror* (1942). It is important to note, however, that the editors of collections of the macabre or the mysterious almost invariably distinguish carefully between ghost stories and tales of horror or suspense. The term "ghost story," says Wells in her foreword, today "mean[s] the clever story, carefully built up and well rounded, that has for its theme a ghost or a mystery, more often than not explained by natural causes. . . . To be sure a mystery story need not contain a ghost at all" (pp. v–vi). These collections commonly feature such psychological dramas as Poe's "The Cask of Amontillado" and "William Wilson," and Bierce's "Occurrence at Owl Creek Bridge." Stern insists that the horror story requires greater skill than the ghost story, for it "attempts to arouse the same heightened emotion without using any ghostly device." Gilman's masterpiece, he says, is "so terrifyingly effective" because it explores "the uncertain area lying along

---

20. *Supernatural Horror in Literature* (New York: Abramson, 1945; reprint New York: Dover, 1973), p. 72.

the edge of sanity where unhinged reason revels with the prodigies of its own spawning" (pp. 16 and 17). Despite their suggestive titles, even Basil Davenport's *Ghostly Tales to be Told* (1950) and Seon Manley and Gogo Lewis's *Ladies of Horror: Two Centuries of Supernatural Stories by the Gentler Sex* (1971), refuse to promote "The Yellow Wall-paper" as a tale of ghosts or supernatural events. Like Wells, Davenport stresses the story's psychological rather than its supernatural dimension, saying that "At ten in the morning, you are not seriously afraid that you will be eaten by a werewolf . . . but you might lose your mind, you know. People do" (p. 238). Manley and Lewis likewise classify the tale as a "psychological horror story." They claim that Gilman "needed no walking ghosts, no monster, no werewolf"; rather, she relied on the knowledge that "those dark sides of our minds give us our own ghosts, our own fears" (p. 137).

Hedges acknowledged the story's continued appeal as a tale of horror and "mental aberration," and called attention to its additional dimension as "a feminist document" (p. 39). Less cautious Gilman scholars suggested that "The Yellow Wallpaper" was valued by its original audience *only* as a horror story or a "spectral tale," without regard to any other possible interpretations. The vague outlines of this reception myth have been darkened and solidified in the apparatus that accompanies the tale in anthologies geared for college students. To give only a few examples, the editors of a 1993 Macmillan collection flatly state that " 'The Yellow Wallpaper' was initially read as a ghost story in the tradition of Edgar Allan Poe." Similarly, the study questions in *The Heath Introduction to Fiction* tell students that " 'The Yellow Wallpaper' was long thought to be a simple 'ghost story.' "[21] By dint of repetition and oversimplification, the legend has become firmly entrenched in Gilman studies, despite the lack of evidence to support it.

Even without the supernatural element, the reception history of "The Yellow Wall-paper" has perpetuated the idea of a dichotomy between Gilman's contemporaries and today's readers. Modern critics, beginning with Hedges, imply an either/or reading of the story: *either* the audience read "The Yellow Wall-paper" as a horror story *or* they read it as a story of sexual politics. The late-nineteenth-century audience, so the mythology goes, read it as horror, but the enlightened readers of a century later see it in its true light. Hedges began this line of interpretation in 1973 with her contention that "no one seems to have made the connection between the insanity and the sex, or sexual role, of the victim, no one explored the story's implications for male-female relationships in the nineteenth century" (Afterword, p. 41).[22] "Not until 1973," says Ann Lane, "was it read from a feminist perspective" (*Gilman Reader*, p. xvii). Lane repeats this claim in her biography of Gilman when she

___

21. *Worlds of Fiction*, ed. Roberta Rubenstein and Charles R. Larson (New York: Macmillan, 1993), p. 387; *Heath Introduction to Fiction*, ed. John J. Clayton (Lexington, Mass.: Heath, 1992), p. 234.

22. Hedges's revised edition of 1996 contains the same assertion, though a new endnote cites my

declares that Hedges's afterword was the "first feminist reading" and that the story "was originally seen as a horror story."[23] Golden echoes Lane: "Howells did not remark in his very brief introduction that 'The Yellow Wallpaper' also 'wanted [more than] two generations' for its feminist thrust or its polemical intent to be appreciated" (*CI*, p. 7). Likewise, the Instructor's Guide for the widely used *Heath Anthology of American Literature* suggests that teachers ask students to consider why the story has "been read as a gothic thriller rather than a story about the sexual politics of marriage."[24]

Yet contemporary reviews demonstrate that the story's first readers did recognize its indictments of marriage and of the treatment of women, even if they did not label them with modern terms like "sexual politics." Three reviews of the 1899 Small, Maynard edition identify the cause of the narrator's insanity as her husband, a man whom one anonymous reviewer calls a "blundering, well-intentioned male murderer" (page 112). Henry B. Blackwell, writing in the *Woman's Journal*, ascribes the narrator's madness to "the effort of her husband," and urges that the book be "perpetuated and widely circulated" (page 107). Another reviewer, in *Time and the Hour*, declares the edition "a book to keep away from the young wife," presumably because the "story is calculated to prevent girls from marrying" (page 108).

We flatter ourselves if we think we are the first to apprehend Gilman's "polemical intent" or her commentary on the sexual politics of marriage in the nineteenth century. Conrad Shumaker observes that Howells for one "understood quite clearly the source of the story's effect" and asserts that the story was unpopular because, as Howells recognized, it "struck too deeply and effectively at traditional ways of seeing the world and woman's place in it."[25] Shumaker's voice has gone unheeded by many feminist critics who, like Haney-Peritz, prefer to generalize about a "male line of response" (*CI*, p. 262). Indeed, it is a male reviewer, Blackwell, who most forcefully makes the point that the narrator's madness results not from any hereditary condition or extraordinary ill-treatment, but rather from the average wife's narrow and isolated life:

> Nothing more graphic and suggestive has ever been written to show why so many women go crazy, especially farmers' wives, who live lonely, monotonous lives. A husband of the kind described in this little sketch once said

---

article and concedes that "since 1973 a few reviews of the 1899 publication of the story have been discovered, which reveal some understanding of the story's sexual politics" (FP2, p. 61).

23. *To Herland and Beyond: The Life and Work of Charlotte Perkins Gilman* (New York: Pantheon, 1990), p. 130.

24. Judith A. Stanford, ed., *Instructor's Guide for the Heath Anthology of American Literature* (Lexington, Mass.: Heath, 1990), p. 349.

25. "'Too Terribly Good to be Printed': Charlotte Gilman's 'The Yellow Wallpaper,'" in Golden, *CI*, p. 251.

that he could not account for his wife's having gone insane—"for," said he, "to my certain knowledge she has hardly left her kitchen and bedroom in 30 years." (page 107)

This either/or interpretation casts nineteenth-century readers as purblind fools insensitive to feminist issues, and implies that only modern readers have the necessary interpretive equipment to read the story appropriately. Jean E. Kennard maintains that a feminist reading of the story could not emerge until audiences grasped certain literary conventions—particularly those associated with "patriarchy, madness, space, [and] quest"—but her premise that "no earlier reader saw the story as in any way positive" obscures the tensions and complexities in Gilman's text, particularly the gender constructions in play between the story and its original readers.[26] To misunderstand these early readers' language of horror as the language of the supernatural is to misinterpret their efforts to read politically in their own times. The story of a female writer going mad and being partially driven there by her husband was indeed a horrifying subject, and not one to be taken lightly. Reviewers recognized its subversive undercurrents, and treated the story with caution. Their remarks might sometimes gloss over the radical social commentary of the story, but the reviews collected in the present volume indicate that Gilman's contemporaries were by no means deaf to her feminist message. Likewise, a brief glance at the list of printings since 1973 reveals that readers in the last quarter of the twentieth century still appreciate the story's chilling qualities, for it has appeared in at least a dozen collections of gothic horror or suspense since feminist critics taught us all how to read it aright.

PERILOUS DOCTORS

If one reception legend portrays nineteenth-century readers as passively insensitive to feminist critiques of the status quo, another paints them as openly antagonistic to such critiques. One of the best-rubbed chestnuts of Gilman criticism concerns the hostility "The Yellow Wall-paper" prompted from her contemporaries, especially the patriarchal medical community. The story made, according to Gilman, a "tremendous impression" (page 87), and even elicited a letter of protest from a Boston physician. Hedges first called modern critics' attention to the warning of "a doctor" that such stories were "perilous stuff" (Afterword, pp. 61, 41), and others have

---

26. "Convention Coverage; or, How to Read Your Own Life," *New Literary History* 11 (1980), 78, 75.

echoed her account.[27] Golden describes how one "protester, an anonymous male physician, argued to censure the story of 'deadly peril'" (*CI*, p. 4), Jeffrey Berman notes the "anger and ill will" of the Boston physician,[28] while Haney-Peritz places him at the head of "a long line of male readers" (*CI*, p. 261).

The source for this entire episode in the story's reception history is the author herself. Explaining "Why I Wrote 'The Yellow Wallpaper'" to readers of *The Forerunner*, Gilman describes the correspondent who wrote to the *Boston Transcript* as "a Boston physician," adding that "he said" stories like hers "ought not to be written" (page 86). Twenty-two years later, she reprints the letter in her autobiography as evidence of the hostility the story initially faced (page 88). With the letter reprinted nicely before us, surely we can trust Gilman's own account. Or can we?

A look at the *Transcript* for 8 April 1892 challenges Gilman's cry of male censorship, as well as the scholarly depictions that derive from it. A letter to the editor entitled "Perilous Stuff" indeed proposes that the vivid portrayal of a woman's mental deterioration is inappropriate subject matter for publication. "Should such stories be allowed to pass without protest, without severest censure?" the pained writer demands (page 103). So far, so good. But the letter includes not the slightest suggestion as to the writer's gender or occupation. Its language merely implies that the writer has a close relationship with a mentally ill person: "The story can hardly, it would seem, give pleasure to any reader, and to many whose lives have been touched through the nearest ties by this dread disease, it must bring the keenest pain." This distress seems more characteristic of a spousal, parental, or sibling relationship than of a doctor-patient relationship, and certainly either sex is capable of such sensitivity. But the writer's identity remains a mystery, for the letter is signed "M. D." The obvious space between the two letters in the *Transcript* text signals that they are initials of a proper name that could as easily have been Margaret Dumont as Michael Douglas (see Fig. 4).

In *The Living*, Gilman chooses to interpret the initials as a doctor's signature. When she reprints the letter she makes slight but significant alterations. Changing "the nearest ties" to "the dearest ties," either by mistake or design, she obscures the implication that the writer and the patient are related. More important, she closes up the space between the crucial initials that sign the letter, presenting the writer as an "M.D." She follows the *Transcript* letter with that of Brummell Jones, whom she identifies as "another doctor," thereby confirming the erroneous impression she has created (page 88).

In relying on Gilman's own account and transcript of the letter, without checking them against the original newspaper, critics have missed the opportunity to consider

27. Since this contention was challenged in my article, Hedges has modified her remarks, eliminating the identification of the letter-writer as "a doctor" (FP2, p. 60).

28. "The Unrestful Cure: Charlotte Perkins Gilman and 'The Yellow Wallpaper,'" in Golden, *CI*, p. 236.

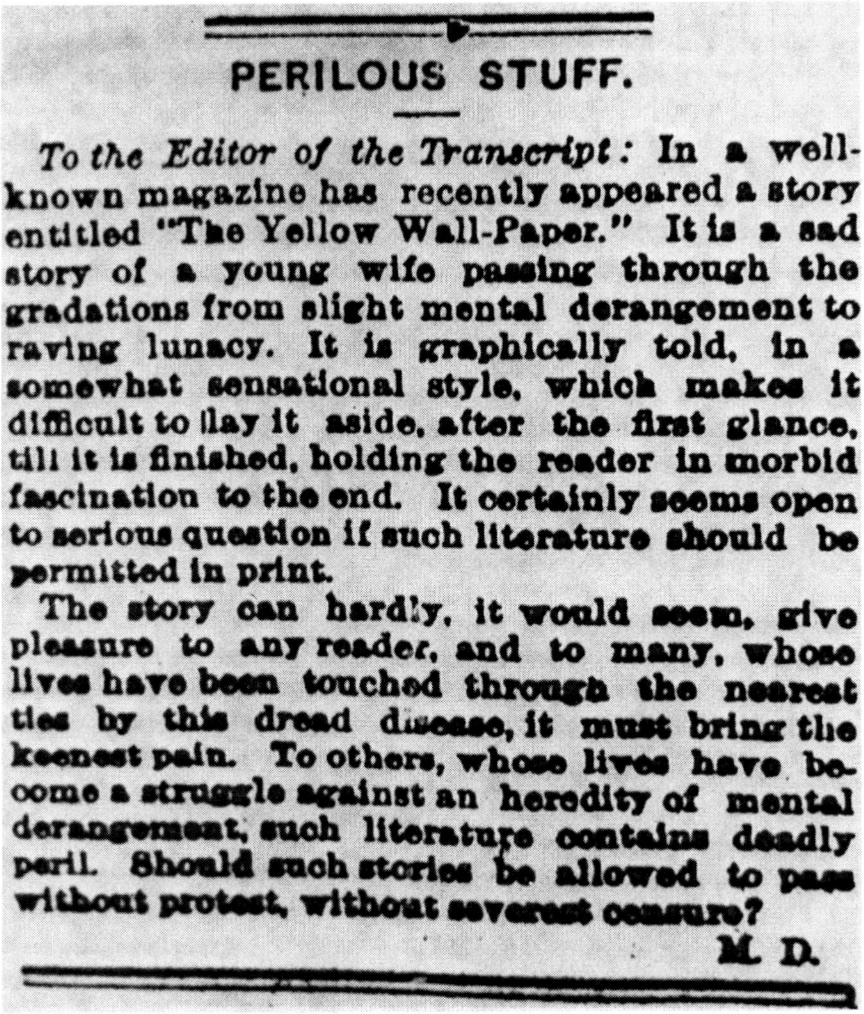

PERILOUS STUFF.

To the Editor of the Transcript: In a well-known magazine has recently appeared a story entitled "The Yellow Wall-Paper." It is a sad story of a young wife passing through the gradations from slight mental derangement to raving lunacy. It is graphically told, in a somewhat sensational style, which makes it difficult to lay it aside, after the first glance, till it is finished, holding the reader in morbid fascination to the end. It certainly seems open to serious question if such literature should be permitted in print.

The story can hardly, it would seem, give pleasure to any reader, and to many, whose lives have been touched through the nearest ties by this dread disease, it must bring the keenest pain. To others, whose lives have become a struggle against an heredity of mental derangement, such literature contains deadly peril. Should such stories be allowed to pass without protest, without severest censure?

M. D.

Fig. 4. M. D., "Perilous Stuff," *Boston Evening Transcript*, 8 April 1892, page 6, column 2.

how Gilman's expectations or motives might have colored her own perception and transmission of the letter. Since her story seems designed to critique common medical practices toward women and the mentally ill, Gilman might have anticipated an angry response from offended doctors and husbands; she might therefore have seen only what she expected to see when she read the letter. Moreover, if the writer *was* a male doctor, he would further exemplify men's continuing attempts to suppress women's creative expression: he would march in lockstep with the male editors whom she claims hindered publication of her story and with the narrator's husband who tries to suppress his wife's writing within the story.

MITCHELL'S CONVERSION

Of course the real villain in the history of "The Yellow Wall-paper" is not some nameless male physician, or even Howells, but the celebrated neurologist Dr. S. Weir Mitchell, at whose hands Gilman herself endured the famous rest cure. What better closure for that troubled history than the knowledge that Gilman's fiction profoundly influenced Mitchell to alter his cure and mend his evil ways? And sure enough, that's what happened—if we believe all we read.

It should by now surprise no one to learn that this apt conclusion originates, once again, with Gilman herself, who develops it through four versions of the story's history that she penned over a period of forty years. An unpublished typescript history of the story refers vaguely to "an eminent specialist in that field [alienism]" who "state[d] that he had changed his treatment of neurasthenia since reading it" (page 85). Gilman's brief essay, "Why I Wrote 'The Yellow Wallpaper,' " published in *The Forerunner* in 1913, twenty years after the story's publication, elaborates on the response of a "noted specialist"—still unnamed—to whom Gilman says she sent a copy of her story. Though he "never acknowledged it," he must have received it, for she notes that "Many years later I was told that the great specialist had admitted to friends of his that he had altered his treatment of neurasthenia since reading *The Yellow Wallpaper.*" The purpose of the story, she adds in this account, was "to save people from being driven crazy, and it worked" (page 86). Gilman makes a similar claim in a letter to W. D. Howells six years later, exclaiming that this was a "Triumph!" Interestingly, the letter shows that she at first overstated the story's impact, writing that Mitchell "told a friend 'I have completely altered my treatement of neurasthenia since reading The Yellow Wallpaper.' " She then crossed out the word "completely," settling for a much lesser claim for the story's effect on Mitchell (see page 96).

In her autobiography, published after a lapse of two more decades, Gilman repeats the tale:

> But the real purpose of the story was to reach Dr. S. Weir Mitchell, and convince him of the error of his ways. I sent him a copy as soon as it came out, but got no response. However, many years later, I met some one who

Fig. 5. Silas Weir Mitchell, c. 1890. Photo by Fr. GuteKunst. Reprinted by permission of the Library of the College of Physicians of Philadelphia.

knew close friends of Dr. Mitchell's who said he had told them that he had changed his treatment of nervous prostration since reading "The Yellow Wallpaper." If that is a fact, I have not lived in vain. (pages 88–89)

Forty years after writing the story, then, Gilman decides that her "real purpose" had been to reach Mitchell, whom she here first publicly identifies by name as her target audience. Moreover, his "friends" become "close friends," lending weight to this thirdhand report of the story's effect. In this final retelling Gilman falls back on melodramatic clichés—"the error of his ways," "I have not lived in vain"—as if to cast herself as the noble heroine who reforms the wicked villain.

Gilman's biographers and critics have taken her story at face value, with no hint of irony. One after another, they reiterate her assertions without commentary or challenge, thereby reinforcing her own highly charged presentation.[29] Even Jeffrey Berman, who brings to bear on his article about "The Unrestful Cure" much research on Mitchell's medical contributions, concludes in Gilman's own ringing tones of triumph. He repeats her report that Mitchell changed his cure, quotes her remark about "sav[ing] people from being crazy" [sic], and adds, "No work of literature can accomplish more than this" (CI, p. 237). Characterizing Mitchell as "a maddeningly self-certain physician," the editors of Wife or Spinster (1991) rejoice that the evil doctor "repent[ed] his horrifying theories on how to treat women in crises, due largely to the influence of Charlotte's tale."[30]

I have found no evidence, other than Gilman's own memoirs, to support her version of events. Discussions of Mitchell's career never mention Gilman—neither her own course of treatment nor her famous short story. Mitchell's published letters and papers contain no hint that he altered his thinking about the rest cure. On the contrary, as late as 1908 he defended his version of the rest treatment before the American Neurological Association, addressing the connections between his methods and the emerging field of psychotherapy.[31] That same year, he wrote to Andrew Carnegie that he wanted to build a hospital for the "Rest Treatment for the Poor."[32] Far from abandoning his methods, he proposed to extend them beyond the middle and upper classes, some sixteen years after Gilman's story appeared.

Additionally, there is no evidence that "The Yellow Wall-paper" discredited either Mitchell or his cure in the eyes of the general public or the medical profession. Indeed, Gilman's own uncle, Edward E. Hale, wrote to Mitchell just six years after the story was first published, asking him to take as a patient a "singularly well educated lady, . . . a human of remarkable range of study and observation." Far from being scared off by Gilman's short story or by his niece's own experience with Mitchell, Hale expressly wished his friend, Miss Freeman, to see Mitchell because, he told the doctor, "you get the confidence of your patients."[33] Aspects of Mitchell's treatment remained widely respected, even by practitioners of the new psycho-

29. Golden anthologizes the work of several critics who lend credence to Gilman's account by their lack of comment upon it. See Golden (p. 8), Parker (p. 84), Gilbert and Gubar (p. 147), Treichler (pp. 199–200), Berman (p. 237), and Jacobus (p. 278). Jacobus alone notes that the story is "hearsay," and she describes Mitchell as a "surrogate for the absent father whom Gilman also tried to 'convert' through her writing."

30. Jessica Amanda Salmonson, Isabelle D. Waugh, and Charles Waugh, eds., Wife or Spinster: Stories by Nineteenth-Century Women (Camden, Maine: Yankee Books, 1991), p. 263.

31. The text of Mitchell's address appears in the Journal of the American Medical Association 50 (1908), 2033–37.

32. Anna Robson, Weir Mitchell: His Life and Letters (New York: Duffield, 1930), p. 344.

33. Hale to Mitchell, 8 May 1898, S. Weir Mitchell Papers, College of Physicians of Philadelphia. Quoted by permission.

therapy who disagreed with his many of his methods. Writing in 1909 about "The Use and Abuse of Rest in the Treatment of Disease," Richard C. Cabot stressed the importance of Mitchell himself in the success of the rest cure:

> Unfortunately, . . . when the medical profession undertook to appropriate and use Dr. Mitchell's treatment for their own patients, they seized upon only one feature, or one or two features, without realizing the *rationale* of the whole, and especially without realizing that Dr. Mitchell's treatment without Dr. Mitchell's personality was a very different and far feebler weapon against disease.[34]

Though Cabot himself advocated what he called the "Work Cure," he valued the rest cure as a first stage in treatment and especially praised Mitchell's insistence on the physician's daily visits with the patient. Acknowledging Mitchell's "rather poor opinion of the word 'psychotherapy' and of those who make much of it," Cabot argued that Mitchell was always "a most brilliant practitioner of this art, and made it, in fact, an essential element in that fundamental reëducation of his patients of which he has said so little and done so much" (p. 26). Recent historians have noted Mitchell's influence on the development of modern psychotherapy and on some of Freud's work. Medical biographer Richard D. Walter writes: "The individual components of the 'rest treatment' have become more fragmented but so completely are they a part of modern medicine that their use is nearly intuitive. . . . The magic ingredient still is what transpires between an interested, unbiased, sympathetic physician and his patient."[35]

*   *   *   *   *   *

The dramatic story of Saint Charlotte and the evil Dr. Mitchell, the indignant outcry of the "Boston physician," the misreading of a searing indictment of marriage as a mere ghost story, the hostility of the male-dominated literary marketplace, the heroic struggles of the undaunted woman author—these critical clichés have gone largely unchallenged for decades. The present collection brings together materials that undercut many of these cherished legends about Gilman and her original audience. This volume includes primary documents—unpublished journal entries, letters, reviews that have not seen print for nearly a century— that provide students and scholars with the materials with which to make their own assessments of the story's publication and reception histories. Much good work has already been done in Gilman criticism, and it is my hope that this collection will provide the fodder for still more fine work from a new generation of scholars.

---

34. *Psychotherapy: A Course of Reading,* vol. 2, no. 2 (1909), p. 26.
35. *S. Weir Mitchell, M.D.—Neurologist: A Medical Biography* (Springfield, Ill: Charles C. Thomas, 1970), p. 203.

The Yellow Wall-paper.

The Yellow Wall-paper.

By *Charlotte Perkins Stetson*.

IT is very seldom that mere ordinary people like John and myself secure ancestral halls for the summer.

A colonial mansion, a hereditary estate, I would say a haunted house, and reach the height of romantic felicity—but that would be asking too much of fate!

Still I will proudly declare that there is something queer about it.

Else, why should it be let so cheaply? And why have stood so long untenanted?

John laughs at me, of course, but one expects that in marriage.

John is practical in the extreme. He has no patience with faith, an intense horror of superstition, and he scoffs openly at any talk of things not to be felt and seen and put down in figures.

John is a physician, and *perhaps*—(I would not say it to a living soul, of course, but this is dead paper and a great relief to my mind)—*perhaps* that is one reason I do not get well faster.

You see he does not believe I am sick!

And what can one do?

If a physician of high standing, and one's own husband, assures friends and relatives that there is really nothing the matter with one but temporary nervous depression—a slight hysterical tendency—what is one to do?

My brother is also a physician, and also of high standing, and he says the same thing.

So I take phosphates or phosphites—whichever it is—and tonics, and journeys, and air, and exercise, and am absolutely forbidden to "work" until I am well again.

Personally, I disagree with their ideas.

Personally, I believe that congenial work, with excitement and change, would do me good.

But what is one to do?

I did write for a while in spite of them; but it *does* exhaust me a good deal—having to be so sly about it, or else meet with heavy opposition.

I sometimes fancy that in my condition if I had less opposition and more society and stimulus—but John says the very worst thing I can do is to think about my condition, and I confess it always makes me feel bad.

So I will let it alone and talk about the house.

The most beautiful place! It is quite alone, standing well back from the road, quite three miles from the village. It makes me think of English places that you read about, for there are hedges and walls and gates that lock, and lots of separate little houses for the gardeners and people.

There is a *delicious* garden! I never saw such a garden—large and shady, full of box-bordered paths, and lined with long grape-covered arbors with seats under them.

There were greenhouses, too, but they are all broken now.

There was some legal trouble, I believe, something about the heirs and co-heirs; anyhow, the place has been empty for years.

That spoils my ghostliness, I am afraid, but I don't care—there is something strange about the house—I can feel it.

I even said so to John one moonlight evening, but he said what I felt was a *draught*, and shut the window.

I get unreasonably angry with John sometimes. I'm sure I never used to be so sensitive. I think it is due to this nervous condition.

But John says if I feel so, I shall neglect proper self-control; so I take pains to control myself—before him, at least, and that makes me very tired.

I don't like our room a bit. I wanted one downstairs that opened on the piazza and had roses all over the window, and such pretty old-fashioned chintz hangings! But John would not hear of it.

He said there was only one window and not room for two beds, and no near room for him if he took another.

He is very careful and loving, and hardly lets me stir without special direction.

I have a schedule prescription for each hour in the day; he takes all care from me, and so I feel basely ungrateful not to value it more.

He said we came here solely on my account, that I was to have perfect rest and all the air I could get. "Your exercise depends on your strength, my dear," said he, "and your food somewhat on your appetite; but air you can absorb all the time." So we took the nursery at the top of the house.

It is a big, airy room, the whole floor nearly, with windows that look all ways, and air and sunshine galore. It was nursery first and then playroom and gymnasium, I should judge; for the windows are barred for little children, and there are rings and things in the walls.

The paint and paper look as if a boys' school had used it. It is stripped off—the paper—in great patches all around the head of my bed, about as far as I can reach, and in a great place on the other side of the room low down. I never saw a worse paper in my life.

One of those sprawling flamboyant patterns committing every artistic sin.

It is dull enough to confuse the eye in following, pronounced enough to constantly irritate and provoke study, and when you follow the lame uncertain curves for a little distance they suddenly commit suicide—plunge off at outrageous angles, destroy themselves in unheard of contradictions.

The color is repellent, almost revolting; a smouldering unclean yellow, strangely faded by the slow-turning sunlight.

It is a dull yet lurid orange in some places, a sickly sulphur tint in others.

No wonder the children hated it! I should hate it myself if I had to live in this room long.

There comes John, and I must put this away—he hates to have me write a word.

★   ★   ★   ★   ★   ★

We have been here two weeks, and I haven't felt like writing before, since that first day.

I am sitting by the window now, up in this atrocious nursery, and there is nothing to hinder my writing as much as I please, save lack of strength.

John is away all day, and even some nights when his cases are serious.

I am glad my case is not serious!

But these nervous troubles are dreadfully depressing.

John does not know how much I really suffer. He knows there is no *reason* to suffer, and that satisfies him.

Of course it is only nervousness. It does weigh on me so not to do my duty in any way!

I meant to be such a help to John, such a real rest and comfort, and here I am a comparative burden already!

Nobody would believe what an effort it is to do what little I am able—to dress and entertain, and order things.

It is fortunate Mary is so good with the baby. Such a dear baby!

And yet I *cannot* be with him, it makes me so nervous.

I suppose John never was nervous in his life. He laughs at me so about this wall-paper!

At first he meant to repaper the room, but afterwards he said that I was letting it get the better of me, and that nothing was worse for a nervous patient than to give way to such fancies.

He said that after the wall-paper was changed it would be the heavy bedstead, and then the barred windows, and then that gate at the head of the stairs, and so on.

"You know the place is doing you good," he said, "and really, dear, I don't care to renovate the house just for a three months' rental."

"Then do let us go downstairs," I said, "there are such pretty rooms there."

Then he took me in his arms and called me a blessed little goose, and said he would go down cellar, if I wished, and have it whitewashed into the bargain.

But he is right enough about the beds and windows and things.

It is as airy and comfortable a room as any one need wish, and, of course, I would not be so silly as to make him uncomfortable just for a whim.

I'm really getting quite fond of the big room, all but that horrid paper.

Out of one window I can see the garden, those mysterious deep-shaded arbors, the riotous old-fashioned flowers, and bushes and gnarly trees.

Out of another I get a lovely view of the bay and a little private wharf belonging to the estate. There is a beautiful shaded lane that runs down there from the house. I always fancy I see people walking in these numerous paths and arbors, but John has cautioned me not to give way to fancy in the least. He says that with my imaginative power and habit of story-making, a nervous weakness like mine is sure to lead to all manner of excited fancies, and that I ought to use my will and good sense to check the tendency. So I try.

I think sometimes that if I were only well enough to write a little it would relieve the press of ideas and rest me.

But I find I get pretty tired when I try.

It is so discouraging not to have any advice and companionship about my work. When I get really well, John says we will ask Cousin Henry and Julia down for a long visit; but he says he would as soon put fireworks in my pillow-case as to let me have those stimulating people about now.

I wish I could get well faster.

But I must not think about that. This paper looks to me as if it *knew* what a vicious influence it had!

There is a recurrent spot where the pattern lolls like a broken neck and two bulbous eyes stare at you upside down.

I get positively angry with the impertinence of it and the everlastingness. Up and down and sideways they crawl, and those absurd, unblinking eyes are everywhere. There is one place where two breadths didn't match, and the eyes go all up and down the line, one a little higher than the other.

I never saw so much expression in an inanimate thing before, and we all know how much expression they have! I used to lie awake as a child and get more entertainment and terror out of blank walls and plain furniture than most children could find in a toy-store.

I remember what a kindly wink the knobs of our big, old bureau used to have, and there was one chair that always seemed like a strong friend.

I used to feel that if any of the other things looked too fierce I could always hop into that chair and be safe.

The furniture in this room is no worse than inharmonious, however, for we had to bring it all from downstairs. I suppose when this was used as a playroom they had to take the nursery things out, and no wonder! I never saw such ravages as the children have made here.

The wall-paper, as I said before, is torn off in spots, and it sticketh closer than a brother[1]—they must have had perseverance as well as hatred.

Then the floor is scratched and gouged and splintered, the plaster itself is dug out here and there, and this great heavy bed, which is all we found in the room, looks as if it had been through the wars.

But I don't mind it a bit—only the paper.

There comes John's sister. Such a dear girl as she is, and so careful of me! I must not let her find me writing.

She is a perfect and enthusiastic housekeeper, and hopes for no better profession. I verily believe she thinks it is the writing which made me sick!

But I can write when she is out, and see her a long way off from these windows.

There is one that commands the road, a lovely shaded winding road, and one that just looks off over the country. A lovely country, too, full of great elms and velvet meadows.

This wall-paper has a kind of sub-pattern in a different shade, a particularly irritating one, for you can only see it in certain lights, and not clearly then.

But in the places where it isn't faded and where the sun is just so—I can see a strange, provoking, formless sort of figure, that seems to skulk about behind that silly and conspicuous front design.

There's sister on the stairs!

*   *   *   *   *   *

Well, the Fourth of July is over! The people are all gone and I am tired out. John thought it might do me good to see a little company, so we just had mother and Nellie and the children down for a week.

Of course I didn't do a thing. Jennie sees to everything now.

But it tired me all the same.

John says if I don't pick up faster he shall send me to Weir Mitchell in the fall.

But I don't want to go there at all. I had a friend who was in his hands once, and she says he is just like John and my brother, only more so!

Besides, it is such an undertaking to go so far.

---

1. **it sticketh closer than a brother** Proverbs 18:24: "There is a friend that sticketh closer than a brother."

I don't feel as if it was worth while to turn my hand over for anything, and I'm getting dreadfully fretful and querulous.

I cry at nothing, and cry most of the time.

Of course I don't when John is here, or anybody else, but when I am alone.

And I am alone a good deal just now. John is kept in town very often by serious cases, and Jennie is good and lets me alone when I want her to.

So I walk a little in the garden or down that lovely lane, sit on the porch under the roses, and lie down up here a good deal.

I'm getting really fond of the room in spite of the wall-paper. Perhaps *because* of the wall-paper.

It dwells in my mind so!

I lie here on this great immovable bed—it is nailed down, I believe—and follow that pattern about by the hour. It is as good as gymnastics, I assure you. I start, we'll say, at the bottom, down in the corner over there where it has not been touched, and I determine for the thousandth time that I *will* follow that pointless pattern to some sort of a conclusion.

I know a little of the principle of design, and I know this thing was not arranged on any laws of radiation, or alternation, or repetition, or symmetry, or anything else that I ever heard of.

It is repeated, of course, by the breadths, but not otherwise.

Looked at in one way each breadth stands alone, the bloated curves and flourishes—a kind of "debased Romanesque" with *delirium tremens*—go waddling up and down in isolated columns of fatuity.

But, on the other hand, they connect diagonally, and the sprawling outlines run off in great slanting waves of optic horror, like a lot of wallowing sea-weeds in full chase.

The whole thing goes horizontally, too, at least it seems so, and I exhaust myself in trying to distinguish the order of its going in that direction.

They have used a horizontal breadth for a frieze, and that adds wonderfully to the confusion.

There is one end of the room where it is almost intact, and there, when the crosslights fade and the low sun shines directly upon it, I can almost fancy radiation after all—the interminable grotesques seem to form around a common centre and rush off in headlong plunges of equal distraction.

It makes me tired to follow it. I will take a nap I guess.

★   ★   ★   ★   ★   ★

I don't know why I should write this.

I don't want to.

I don't feel able.

And I know John would think it absurd. But I *must* say what I feel and think in some way—it is such a relief!

But the effort is getting to be greater than the relief.

Half the time now I am awfully lazy, and lie down ever so much.

John says I mustn't lose my strength, and has me take cod liver oil and lots of tonics and things, to say nothing of ale and wine and rare meat.

Dear John! He loves me very dearly, and hates to have me sick. I tried to have a real earnest reasonable talk with him the other day, and tell him how I wish he would let me go and make a visit to Cousin Henry and Julia.

But he said I wasn't able to go, nor able to stand it after I got there; and I did not make out a very good case for myself, for I was crying before I had finished.

It is getting to be a great effort for me to think straight. Just this nervous weakness I suppose.

And dear John gathered me up in his arms, and just carried me upstairs and laid me on the bed, and sat by me and read to me till it tired my head.

He said I was his darling and his comfort and all he had, and that I must take care of myself for his sake, and keep well.

He says no one but myself can help me out of it, that I must use my will and self-control and not let any silly fancies run away with me.

There's one comfort, the baby is well and happy, and does not have to occupy this nursery with the horrid wall-paper.

If we had not used it, that blessed child would have! What a fortunate escape! Why, I wouldn't have a child of mine, an impressionable little thing, live in such a room for worlds.

I never thought of it before, but it is lucky that John kept me here after all, I can stand it so much easier than a baby, you see.

Of course I never mention it to them any more—I am too wise—but I keep watch of it all the same.

There are things in that paper that nobody knows but me, or ever will.

Behind that outside pattern the dim shapes get clearer every day.

It is always the same shape, only very numerous.

And it is like a woman stooping down and creeping about behind that pattern. I don't like it a bit. I wonder—I begin to think—I wish John would take me away from here!

* * * * * *

It is so hard to talk with John about my case, because he is so wise, and because he loves me so.

But I tried it last night.

It was moonlight. The moon shines in all around just as the sun does.

I hate to see it sometimes, it creeps so slowly, and always comes in by one window or another.

John was asleep and I hated to waken him, so I kept still and watched the moonlight on that undulating wall-paper till I felt creepy.

The faint figure behind seemed to shake the pattern, just as if she wanted to get out.

I got up softly and went to feel and see if the paper *did* move, and when I came back John was awake.

"What is it, little girl?" he said. "Don't go walking about like that—you'll get cold."

I thought it was a good time to talk, so I told him that I really was not gaining here, and that I wished he would take me away.

"Why, darling!" said he, "our lease will be up in three weeks, and I can't see how to leave before.

"The repairs are not done at home, and I cannot possibly leave town just now. Of course if you were in any danger, I could and would, but you really are better, dear, whether you can see it or not. I am a doctor, dear, and I know. You are gaining flesh and color, your appetite is better, I feel really much easier about you."

"I don't weigh a bit more," said I, "nor as much; and my appetite may be better in the evening when you are here, but it is worse in the morning when you are away!"

"Bless her little heart!" said he with a big hug, "she shall be as sick as she pleases! But now let's improve the shining hours[2] by going to sleep, and talk about it in the morning!"

"And you won't go away?" I asked gloomily.

"Why, how can I, dear? It is only three weeks more and then we will take a nice little trip of a few days while Jennie is getting the house ready. Really, dear, you are better!"

"Better in body perhaps—" I began, and stopped short, for he sat up straight and looked at me with such a stern, reproachful look that I could not say another word.

"My darling," said he, "I beg of you, for my sake and for our child's sake, as well as for your own, that you will never for one instant let that idea enter your mind! There is nothing so dangerous, so fascinating, to a temperament like yours. It is a false and foolish fancy. Can you not trust me as a physician when I tell you so?"

So of course I said no more on that score, and we went to sleep before long. He

---

2. **let's improve the shining hours** In his poem "Against Idleness and Mischief," Isaac Watts (1674–1748) writes:

> How doth the little busy bee
> Improve each shining hour,
> And gather honey all the day
> From every opening flower!

thought I was asleep first, but I wasn't, and lay there for hours trying to decide whether that front pattern and the back pattern really did move together or separately.

★   ★   ★   ★   ★   ★

On a pattern like this, by daylight, there is a lack of sequence, a defiance of law, that is a constant irritant to a normal mind.

The color is hideous enough, and unreliable enough, and infuriating enough, but the pattern is torturing.

You think you have mastered it, but just as you get well underway in following, it turns a back-somersault and there you are. It slaps you in the face, knocks you down, and tramples upon you. It is like a bad dream.

The outside pattern is a florid arabesque, reminding one of a fungus. If you can imagine a toadstool in joints, an interminable string of toadstools, budding and sprouting in endless convolutions—why, that is something like it.

That is, sometimes!

There is one marked peculiarity about this paper, a thing nobody seems to notice but myself, and that is that it changes as the light changes.

When the sun shoots in through the east window—I always watch for that first long, straight ray—it changes so quickly that I never can quite believe it.

That is why I watch it always.

By moonlight—the moon shines in all night when there is a moon—I wouldn't know it was the same paper.

At night in any kind of light, in twilight, candlelight, lamplight, and worst of all by moonlight, it becomes bars! The outside pattern, I mean, and the woman behind it is as plain as can be.

I didn't realize for a long time what the thing was that showed behind, that dim sub-pattern, but now I am quite sure it is a woman.

By daylight she is subdued, quiet. I fancy it is the pattern that keeps her so still. It is so puzzling. It keeps me quiet by the hour.

I lie down ever so much now. John says it is good for me, and to sleep all I can.

Indeed he started the habit by making me lie down for an hour after each meal.

It is a very bad habit, I am convinced, for you see I don't sleep.

And that cultivates deceit, for I don't tell them I'm awake—O no!

The fact is I am getting a little afraid of John.

He seems very queer sometimes, and even Jennie has an inexplicable look.

It strikes me occasionally, just as a scientific hypothesis, that perhaps it is the paper!

I have watched John when he did not know I was looking, and come into the room suddenly on the most innocent excuses, and I've caught him several times *looking at the paper!* And Jennie too. I caught Jennie with her hand on it once.

She didn't know I was in the room, and when I asked her in a quiet, a very quiet voice, with the most restrained manner possible, what she was doing with the paper—she turned around as if she had been caught stealing, and looked quite angry—asked me why I should frighten her so!

Then she said that the paper stained everything it touched, that she had found yellow smooches on all my clothes and John's, and she wished we would be more careful!

Did not that sound innocent? But I know she was studying that pattern, and I am determined that nobody shall find it out but myself!

★   ★   ★   ★   ★   ★

Life is very much more exciting now than it used to be. You see I have something more to expect, to look forward to, to watch. I really do eat better, and am more quiet than I was.

John is so pleased to see me improve! He laughed a little the other day, and said I seemed to be flourishing in spite of my wall-paper.

I turned it off with a laugh. I had no intention of telling him it was *because* of the wall-paper—he would make fun of me. He might even want to take me away.

I don't want to leave now until I have found it out. There is a week more, and I think that will be enough.

★   ★   ★   ★   ★   ★

I'm feeling ever so much better! I don't sleep much at night, for it is so interesting to watch developments; but I sleep a good deal in the daytime.

In the daytime it is tiresome and perplexing.

There are always new shoots on the fungus, and new shades of yellow all over it. I cannot keep count of them, though I have tried conscientiously.

It is the strangest yellow, that wall-paper! It makes me think of all the yellow things I ever saw—not beautiful ones like buttercups, but old foul, bad yellow things.

But there is something else about that paper—the smell! I noticed it the moment we came into the room, but with so much air and sun it was not bad. Now we have had a week of fog and rain, and whether the windows are open or not, the smell is here.

It creeps all over the house.

I find it hovering in the dining-room, skulking in the parlor, hiding in the hall, lying in wait for me on the stairs.

It gets into my hair.

Even when I go to ride, if I turn my head suddenly and surprise it—there is that smell!

Such a peculiar odor, too! I have spent hours in trying to analyze it, to find what it smelled like.

It is not bad—at first—and very gentle, but quite the subtlest, most enduring odor I ever met.

In this damp weather it is awful, I wake up in the night and find it hanging over me.

It used to disturb me at first. I thought seriously of burning the house—to reach the smell.

But now I am used to it. The only thing I can think of that it is like is the *color* of the paper! A yellow smell.

There is a very funny mark on this wall, low down, near the mopboard. A streak that runs round the room. It goes behind every piece of furniture, except the bed, a long, straight, even *smooch,* as if it had been rubbed over and over.

I wonder how it was done and who did it, and what they did it for. Round and round and round—round and round and round—it makes me dizzy!

★   ★   ★   ★   ★   ★

I really have discovered something at last.

Through watching so much at night, when it changes so, I have finally found out. The front pattern *does* move—and no wonder! The woman behind shakes it!

Sometimes I think there are a great many women behind, and sometimes only one, and she crawls around fast, and her crawling shakes it all over.

Then in the very bright spots she keeps still, and in the very shady spots she just takes hold of the bars and shakes them hard.

And she is all the time trying to climb through. But nobody could climb through that pattern—it strangles so; I think that is why it has so many heads.

They get through, and then the pattern strangles them off and turns them upside down, and makes their eyes white!

If those heads were covered or taken off it would not be half so bad.

★   ★   ★   ★   ★   ★

I think that woman gets out in the daytime!

And I'll tell you why—privately—I've seen her!

I can see her out of every one of my windows!

It is the same woman, I know, for she is always creeping, and most women do not creep by daylight.

I see her in that long shaded lane, creeping up and down. I see her in those dark grape arbors, creeping all around the garden.

I see her on that long road under the trees, creeping along, and when a carriage comes she hides under the blackberry vines.

I don't blame her a bit. It must be very humiliating to be caught creeping by daylight!

I always lock the door when I creep by daylight. I can't do it at night, for I know John would suspect something at once.

And John is so queer now, that I don't want to irritate him. I wish he would take another room! Besides, I don't want anybody to get that woman out at night but myself.

I often wonder if I could see her out of all the windows at once.

But, turn as fast as I can, I can only see out of one at one time.

And though I always see her, she *may* be able to creep faster than I can turn!

I have watched her sometimes away off in the open country, creeping as fast as a cloud shadow in a high wind.

⋆　⋆　⋆　⋆　⋆　⋆

If only that top pattern could be gotten off from the under one! I mean to try it, little by little.

I have found out another funny thing, but I shan't tell it this time! It does not do to trust people too much.

There are only two more days to get this paper off, and I believe John is beginning to notice. I don't like the look in his eyes.

And I heard him ask Jennie a lot of professional questions about me. She had a very good report to give.

She said I slept a good deal in the daytime.

John knows I don't sleep very well at night, for all I'm so quiet!

He asked me all sorts of questions, too, and pretended to be very loving and kind. As if I couldn't see through him!

Still, I don't wonder he acts so, sleeping under this paper for three months.

It only interests me, but I feel sure John and Jennie are secretly affected by it.

⋆　⋆　⋆　⋆　⋆　⋆

Hurrah! This is the last day, but it is enough. John had to stay in town over night, and won't be out until this evening.

Jennie wanted to sleep with me—the sly thing!—but I told her I should undoubtedly rest better for a night all alone.

That was clever, for really I wasn't alone a bit! As soon as it was moonlight and that poor thing began to crawl and shake the pattern, I got up and ran to help her.

I pulled and she shook, I shook and she pulled, and before morning we had peeled off yards of that paper.

A strip about as high as my head and half around the room.

And then when the sun came and that awful pattern began to laugh at me, I declared I would finish it to-day!

We go away to-morrow, and they are moving all my furniture down again to leave things as they were before.

Jennie looked at the wall in amazement, but I told her merrily that I did it out of pure spite at the vicious thing.

She laughed and said she wouldn't mind doing it herself, but I must not get tired. How she betrayed herself that time!

But I am here, and no person touches this paper but me—not *alive!*

She tried to get me out of the room—it was too patent! But I said it was so quiet and empty and clean now that I believed I would lie down again and sleep all I could; and not to wake me even for dinner—I would call when I woke.

So now she is gone, and the servants are gone, and the things are gone, and there is nothing left but that great bedstead nailed down, with the canvas mattress we found on it.

We shall sleep downstairs to-night, and take the boat home to-morrow.

I quite enjoy the room, now it is bare again.

How those children did tear about here!

This bedstead is fairly gnawed!

But I must get to work.

I have locked the door and thrown the key down into the front path.

I don't want to go out, and I don't want to have anybody come in, till John comes.

I want to astonish him.

I've got a rope up here that even Jennie did not find. If that woman does get out, and tries to get away, I can tie her!

But I forgot I could not reach far without anything to stand on!

This bed will *not* move!

I tried to lift and push it until I was lame, and then I got so angry I bit off a little piece at one corner—but it hurt my teeth.

Then I peeled off all the paper I could reach standing on the floor. It sticks horribly and the pattern just enjoys it! All those strangled heads and bulbous eyes and waddling fungus growths just shriek with derision!

I am getting angry enough to do something desperate. To jump out of the window would be admirable exercise, but the bars are too strong even to try.

Besides, I wouldn't do it. Of course not. I know well enough that a step like that is improper and might be misconstrued.

I don't like to *look* out of the windows even—there are so many of those creeping women, and they creep so fast.

I wonder if they all come out of that wall-paper as I did?

But I am securely fastened now by my well-hidden rope—you don't get *me* out in the road there!

I suppose I shall have to get back behind the pattern when it comes night, and that is hard!

It is so pleasant to be out in this great room and creep around as I please!

I don't want to go outside. I won't, even if Jennie asks me to.

For outside you have to creep on the ground, and everything is green instead of yellow.

But here I can creep smoothly on the floor, and my shoulder just fits in that long smooch around the wall, so I cannot lose my way.

Why, there's John at the door!

It is no use, young man, you can't open it!

How he does call and pound!

Now he's crying for an axe.

It would be a shame to break down that beautiful door!

"John, dear!" said I in the gentlest voice, "the key is down by the front steps, under a plantain leaf!"

That silenced him for a few moments.

Then he said—very quietly indeed—"Open the door, my darling!"

"I can't," said I. "The key is down by the front door under a plantain leaf!"

And then I said it again, several times, very gently and slowly, and said it so often that he had to go and see, and he got it of course, and came in. He stopped short by the door.

"What is the matter?" he cried. "For God's sake, what are you doing!"

I kept on creeping just the same, but I looked at him over my shoulder.

"I've got out at last," said I, "in spite of you and Jane! And I've pulled off most of the paper, so you can't put me back!"

Now why should that man have fainted? But he did, and right across my path by the wall, so that I had to creep over him every time!

Textual Notes

COMMENTARY

SELECTION OF COPY-TEXT

Editorial theory has undergone significant change in the past few decades, especially with respect to modern works for which prepublication documents exist. The dominant school of textual editing for most of this century descends from the work of W. W. Greg and Fredson Bowers. These editors developed their methodology in the arena of premodern texts, where multiple published versions exist but prepublication documents (such as authorial manuscripts or corrected proofs) are rare. An editor in this tradition aims to reconstruct the author's lost original by purging the text of the corruptions that have accrued through multiple editions and printings. Typically, an editor will choose one text on which to base his or her own and then introduce into that base text, or "copy-text," such emendations and corrections as are necessary to restore the work as nearly as possible to the author's no longer extant original. Greg's famous "Rationale of Copy-Text" maintained that "the copy-text should govern (generally) in the matter of accidentals," that is in the spelling and punctuation of the text, the bibliographic form in which it is offered to the reader.[1] For variants of wording Greg used the term "substantives," and directed that with this class of variants the editor must apply the general principles of textual criticism to determine which reading can best be deemed "authorial." If there is no clear choice among substantives supplied by different texts, if the readings are what Greg calls

---

1. W. W. Greg, "The Rationale of Copy-Text," *The Collected Papers of Sir Walter W. Greg*, ed. J. C. Maxwell (Oxford: Oxford University Press, 1966), p. 377.

"indifferent," then the reading found in the copy-text remains unemended. This approach to textual editing produces "eclectic texts" that blend readings from different versions, recording all textual variants in an apparatus that accompanies the critical text.

Editors applying this method to modern texts generally (though not invariably) select an authorial manuscript as their copy-text, if one survives, on the principle that the manuscript best represents authorial practices that might have been skewed by printing-house treatment. Jerome McGann first called this methodology into question with his *Critique of Modern Textual Criticism* (1980), and he has since elaborated on his ideas, as have others. Arguing that "literary texts, and their meanings, are collaborative events," McGann suggests that editors adopt what has come to be called the "social theory" of textual editing.[2] He maintains that editors should recognize the essentially interactive nature of texts as communicative events that involve authors, printers, readers, and others in a complex network of social relations. Where editors of the Greg-Bowers school aim to disclose the author's "final intentions" by stripping the text of editorial corruptions, McGann argues that editorial intervention might have been an integral part of an author's intentions in laying his or her work before the public. Moreover, there might have been no "final" intention, but rather a plethora of intentions, each influenced to a differing degree by the author's interaction with readers, editors, and publishers. Thus even if it were possible to isolate an author's final intentions, those intentions should not become "the ultimate and determining criterion for copy-text" ("Critical Editing," p. 24). Editors must instead take account of the multiple authorities that influenced the text's transmission, from the author's dominant but not exclusive authority over the "linguistic text" (the words of the literary work) to the editor's and publisher's dominant but not exclusive authority over the "bibliographic text" (the presentation in printed form of the literary work).

The varying texts of Charlotte Perkins Gilman's short story "The Yellow Wallpaper" present the paradigmatic situation addressed by the current debate in textual criticism. The story exists in seven published versions authorized during the author's lifetime: the 1892 printing in *The New England Magazine* (NE); a monograph published in 1899 by Small, Maynard & Co. (SM); an anthology compiled by William Dean Howells in 1920, *Great Modern American Stories* (WDH); a reprint in the *New York Evening Post,* 21 January 1922; Carolyn Wells's 1927 collection *American Mystery Stories* (CW); another reprint in *The Golden Book Magazine*, October 1933 (GB); and a final reprint in a college literature anthology assembled by E. A. Cross in 1934. In addition to these published versions, the story survives in a manuscript in the author's own hand (AMS), located in the Charlotte Perkins

---

2. "What is Critical Editing?" *Text: Transactions of the Society for Textual Scholarship* 5 (1991), 23.

Gilman Papers of the Schlesinger Library at Radcliffe College. The textual editor's task must be to determine which, if any, of these eight texts should be considered most "authoritative." Should any one version have priority? Or would the ideal text be an eclectic blend of several versions?

Editions of the story since its rediscovery by literary critics in the 1970s present texts that follow one or another (or sometimes several) of the available versions, often introducing new variants inadvertently. These editions generally lack any explicit textual/critical rationale. In her 1973 edition (FP), Elaine Hedges republishes the 1892 magazine version, but her faithful rendering is marred by several typographical errors—including the omission of two lines—as well as the mislabelling of her version as the 1899 Small, Maynard text. In 1996 the Feminist Press issued a revised edition (FP2) that corrects these errors and presents "A Complete and Accurate Rendition of the 1892 Edition, with a New Note on the Text." Hedges's brief textual note announces that the new edition "reprints the story exactly as it appeared in its first published form in *New England Magazine* in January 1892, except for the correction of typographical errors in that publication" (p. 7). Ann Lane's *Charlotte Perkins Gilman Reader* (GR) offers a text that largely follows *The Golden Book's* idiosyncratic version, but is identified as the 1892 magazine text. In their volume in the Rutgers University Press series Women Writers: Texts and Contexts, editors Thomas Erskine and Connie Richards randomly combine Lane's and Hedges's texts to present what they claim is "the authoritative text" of "The Yellow Wall-paper" (WW), but they do so without indicating the sources of their readings or the bases for their editorial choices. The scholar who addresses textual matters most directly is Denise D. Knight, editor of *"The Yellow Wall-Paper" and Selected Stories of Charlotte Perkins Gilman* (1994). She presents a transcription of the "original manuscript," investing that choice of text with the implication that the manuscript best represents Gilman's uncorrupted intentions. Knight records sixteen "discrepancies" between the manuscript and the story's first appearance in print that "seem particularly noteworthy," and she explains that her "objective has been to preserve, rather than to correct or amend, Gilman's original text."[3] None of these editions presents the range of variants that exists among the eight versions, nor do the editors attempt to ascertain the relative authority of the various printed versions.

Faced with these varying texts of "The Yellow Wall-paper," a critical editor following the Greg-Bowers methodology might adopt the manuscript as copy-text, acting on the assumption that the manuscript was the basis for the later printed versions. This copy-text would then be emended with later variants that could be reasonably deemed authoritative (corrections in proof or revisions occasioned by

---

3. *"The Yellow Wall-Paper" and Selected Stories of Charlotte Perkins Gilman* (Newark: University of Delaware Press, 1994), pp. 223 and 33. Knight's transcription contains a few inaccuracies, which I have noted in my introduction to the list of Pre-copy-text Substantive Variants (page 71).

book publication, for instance, should such evidence be discovered). The resulting eclectic text would offer the reader the editor's best estimate as to the author's "final intention" for her story. The present edition offers an eclectic text, but I have taken a different approach: copy-text for this edition is the first published version of the story (NE), rather than the manuscript, for reasons discussed below. This text is emended as necessary with readings from the manuscript in the case of substantive variants, and according to principles detailed in the editorial apparatus, in the case of accidentals. Thus I am not presenting an exact transcription of NE or any other version of "The Yellow Wall-paper" that has previously existed. I am instead offering the reader my best estimate of the story as Gilman might have expected her first audience to read it. I also offer a full record of the variants among the editions that textual analysis has discovered to be of importance to the transmission of the text of "The Yellow Wall-paper." Readers may reconstruct any of the relevant texts from these lists of variants, should they wish to do so.

In selecting NE as the copy-text for this edition, I have weighed several considerations, including the manuscript's authority, the story's publication history, Gilman's authorial practice, and her attitude toward editorial alteration of her works. Since this volume also presents documents illustrative of the original audience's reception of the story, I have paid heed to which version Gilman's contemporaries would have been familiar with. That is to say, I have borne in mind my own readers' needs and interests as well as those of Gilman's readers. The discussion below outlines these matters and lays out my editorial procedures and rationale.

Gilman's manuscript

The surviving manuscript of "The Yellow Wall-paper" is a fair copy in Gilman's hand that was, presumably, sent to editors in hopes of publication. The author has indicated her name and the approximate length of the story at the top of the first page, and she has given instructions for the return of the manuscript if it was deemed unsuited for publication. But there is reason to doubt whether this manuscript was the printer's copy for NE, the first printing of the story and the basis for all subsequent editions.

Evidence suggests that Gilman made at least two fair copies. Her manuscript log records that on 14 June 1890 she sent "The Yellow Wall-paper" to *Scribner's Magazine*. She was a sufficiently professional author even at this early point in her career that she would not have been likely to offer a foul draft of her story for publication consideration. If we accept this assumption, then she must have made one fair copy prior to 14 June. The log entry is crossed out, either because she changed her mind and did not send the story out or, more likely, because *Scribner's* rejected it. Regardless of which is the case, her very intention to send the manuscript would almost certainly have caused her to produce a fair copy of the story by mid-June 1890. According to Gilman's diary, another fair copy was finished on 24 August 1890, just three days before she sent the story to Howells, asking him to pass it on to Horace Scudder. In mid-October, when Scudder rejected the story for publication in *The Atlantic Monthly*, he returned the manuscript to Gilman, along with a note of rejection written on a card inserted into the package containing the manuscript (see page 91).

Less than a week after receiving Scudder's rejection, Gilman sent "The Yellow Wall-paper" to the literary agent Henry Austin (26 October 1890). Fourteen months later, the story was published in the January 1892 issue of *The New England Magazine*, presumably in a version typeset from a fair copy manuscript. During those fourteen months, Gilman read "The Yellow Wall-paper" aloud to friends and family on at least three occasions (see pages 82–85). She read either from her original draft of the story or from a fair copy that she retained while a second one was circulating among editors. Her reading copy may have been the first fair copy, after it had been returned by *Scribner's*.

Gilman's recollections of her dealings with *The New England Magazine* also support the idea that a second manuscript existed. She claims in her autobiography that after the story was published, "Time passed, much time," during which she received no payment for the story; after more than six months had elapsed, she says, she wrote to the editor to ask when she would be paid (page 87). Had the magazine returned her manuscript during that time, would not Gilman be likely to reply immediately about the overdue payment, especially since her livelihood in 1892 was so heavily dependent on her writing and lecturing revenues? The same magazine had published Gilman's story "The Giant Wistaria" in its June 1891 issue (fifteen months after she had submitted it "via Walter"), and two months later she recorded in her diary a payment of $14 for that story. Nevertheless, in the letter she reprints in *The Living* regarding "The Yellow Wall-paper," Gilman claims ignorance of the magazine's payment policy.

It is probable that the manuscript in Gilman's archive was not the one from which the first printing of the story was set. It contains a number of readings that differ from the 1892 *New England Magazine* text in ways that do not suggest simple misreading of the manuscript by compositors, such as the substitution of "humiliating" for the manuscript's reading "unpleasant" at 39.37 or the addition of the final two words of the story, which do not appear in AMS. Moreover, the manuscript contains no stab marks or printer's notations that would substantiate its use as printer's copy. If the chronology I have proposed is correct, the manuscript that survives might represent a state of the story dating from June 1890, when she made the fair copy for *Scribner's*. It is possible that this was also the manuscript from which Gilman read aloud after sending the other manuscript to Austin; the few insertions in the manuscript would then represent revisions that arose as she read the story to an audience. Whichever is the case, we need not automatically grant the manuscript highest priority and regard the printed versions as departures from the author's "true" intentions. Instead, we may regard it as a distinct "version" of "The Yellow Wall-paper," in McGann's terminology, one that represents a different (perhaps earlier, perhaps later) authorial intention than NE. Editors in the Bowers and McGann traditions would agree that AMS deserves consideration in the choice of copy-text, but not to the exclusion of other witnesses.

Publication history

"The Yellow Wall-paper" first appeared in print in the January 1892 issue of *New England Magazine* (NE). Following the chronology set forth above, it seems possible that NE was set from another manuscript of the story than the one that survives today. Textual evidence bolsters such a possibility. Many of the discrepancies between NE and AMS can be attributed to editorial conventions. For instance, NE consistently expands the contractions that appear in AMS (as at 29.13), corrects Gilman's grammar (30.5) and eliminates narrative inconsistencies (35.22). NE also renders underlined words in roman rather than italic type with nearly equal consistency. However, printing-house regularization of an inconsistent manuscript fails to explain many of the variants recorded in the list of "Pre-copy-text Substantive Variants." Nor can they be blamed on any illegibility of AMS. Such substantives as "frieze" for the manuscript's "border" (34.29), "humiliating" for "unpleasant" (39.37), or the omission of "A sickly penetrating suggestive yellow" (38.25) can be explained in two ways: either the editors at *The New England Magazine* wielded a heavy hand at revision, or the magazine's compositor set type from a different manuscript than AMS. (For other examples, see the readings at 30.6, 30.16, 30.31, 32.20, 35.4, 38.16, 38.28, 41.9, 42.9, and 42.23.) Authorial revision can be seen clearly at two points in the surviving manuscript: at 35.14 the manuscript reads "his strong arms"—with the word "strong" inserted in Gilman's hand—and NE prints "his arms"; and at 42.14 the manuscript reads "front ~~door~~ steps" and NE prints "front door". Neither the author's insertion nor her deletion appears in the magazine text of the story. Barring willful defiance of authorial instructions on the part of the compositor, these changes suggest, again, that the compositor read from a different manuscript than the one that survives. These discrepancies could also be accounted for if Gilman made the changes after the manuscript was returned to her, following its publication in *The New England Magazine,* perhaps in preparation for book publication of the story. This supposition would be more tenable if the author's revisions showed up in SM, but they do not. Moreover, as I shall show, Gilman's attitudes toward publication and toward "The Yellow Wall-paper" mili-

"I am sitting by the Window in this Atrocious Nursery."

THE YELLOW WALL–PAPER.

By Charlotte Perkins Stetson.

IT is very seldom that mere ordinary people like John and myself secure ancestral halls for the summer.

A colonial mansion, a hereditary estate, I would say a haunted house, and reach the height of romantic felicity—but that would be asking too much of fate!

Still I will proudly declare that there is something queer about it.

Else, why should it be let so cheaply? And why have stood so long untenanted?

John laughs at me, of course, but one expects that in marriage.

John is practical in the extreme. He has no patience with faith, an intense horror of superstition, and he scoffs openly at any talk of things not to be felt and seen and put down in figures.

John is a physician, and *perhaps*— (I would not say it to a living soul, of course, but this is dead paper and a great relief to my mind—) *perhaps* that is one reason I do not get well faster.

You see he does not believe I am sick! And what can one do?

Fig. 6. "The Yellow Wall-paper," *The New England Magazine*, January 1892, p. 647.

tate against the notion of any meticulous revision of the story once it had been published.

Small, Maynard & Co. of Boston issued *The Yellow Wall Paper* (SM) in June 1899, and this monograph version presents a curious mixture of textual evidence that suggests both a collateral and derivative relationship to NE.[4] SM follows NE in nearly all substantive readings, though it departs from NE in many accidentals. In several instances, SM corrects a faulty NE reading and produces a reading that matches AMS. At 32.7, NE's "an airy and comfortable room" returns to the manuscript's "as airy and comfortable a room"; likewise "breaths" returns to AMS's "breadths" at 32.33, and "grotesque" returns to "grotesques" at 34.33. Any of these readings could have been arrived at without consulting AMS, however, for all restore grammatical or logical sense to the text; additionally, the same variants appear in other texts that almost certainly were not set from AMS. In three substantives, however, SM stands alone among the printed texts in matching AMS: when the narrator describes Jennie as "a perfect, an enthusiastic housekeeper" (33.15), remarks that she knows "a little of the principles of design" (34.17), and claims that John "thought I was asleep first, but I wasn't,—I lay there for hours" (37.1), SM coincides with AMS, rather than reproducing the perfectly acceptable readings found in NE. In spite of these intriguing matches, there is little likelihood that SM derives from AMS, for too many other substantives depart from the manuscript and match the magazine's readings. (Compare such pre-copy-text variants as those at 30.7, 30.16, 34.29, 35.4, 38.25, 38.28, or 39.37.) The accidentals give little indication of SM's origin, for they often depart from all other versions. SM's style includes the frequent use of the comma and dash together, as well as the insertion of commas to set off interjections. At times, these tendencies coincide with Gilman's punctuation in AMS, but just as often they do not. Similarly, SM introduces new substantive readings at 30.38, 32.31, 33.24, 35.8, 35.15, 35.19, and 39.10 that appear in neither AMS nor any of the printed texts. Yet none of these new readings differs from NE by more than a few letters, suggesting that these could have been simple mistranscriptions of NE on the part of SM's compositor. If SM was set from any manuscript, it was set from the same one as NE. However, it seems more likely that SM derives directly, if freely, from NE.

---

4. The story was said to be "in preparation" in the 13 May 1899 number of *Publishers' Weekly* (p. 788). It was the last item in Small, Maynard's "Spring Announcement List" in the same journal's Summer Reading issue of 27 May (p. 834); there the publisher touts the book as "A story which has already taken rank (in the opinion of the comparatively few to whom it is familiar) in the same class as the tales of Edgar Allan Poe." On 17 June 1899, *The Yellow Wall Paper* appears in the journal's weekly record of books printed, accompanied by the following capsule description, probably supplied by Small, Maynard: "A story depicting a woman's gradual mental unbalancing: she goes with her husband to a quiet country place for rest and sleeps in a room papered with a hideous yellow paper; her mind dwells upon its ugliness and she imagines things about it, till she becomes insane" (p. 974).

Fig. 7. Cover of *The Yellow Wall Paper* (Boston: Small, Maynard & Company, 1899). Courtesy of the Huntington Library, San Marino, California.

THE
YELLOW WALL PAPER

BY

CHARLOTTE PERKINS STETSON

SCIRE QVOD
SCIENDVM

BOSTON

SMALL, MAYNARD & COMPANY

MDCCCXCIX

Fig. 8. Title page of *The Yellow Wall Paper* (Boston: Small, Maynard & Company, 1899). Courtesy of the Huntington Library, San Marino, California.

We have no evidence to support or refute the notion that, like many another author, Gilman revised her story between its appearances in magazine and book form. Small, Maynard apparently made plans to publish *The Yellow Wall Paper* only after *In This Our World* and *Women and Economics* had begun to show some success. During the six weeks Gilman spent in Boston in the fall of 1898, she visited her publisher several times and received encouraging news about the strong sales of her first two books. On 2 November 1898 she and Herbert Small discussed a possible book of short stories. Writing to George Houghton Gilman, she describes that meeting:

> I told him the drift of several I had in mind, they growing in vividness as I described them, winding up with The Price of Love. He was "spell-bound"—[illeg.] doubly impressed. Wants a book of 4 or 5000 words— perhaps 8 or 10 stories—or less—the collection I've had in mind for some time, to be called "Their Shadows Before". Palpable "stories with a pur-pose" but popular along the very line my book is going—the new house-keeping. He is eager for the stuff. So am I. I'll sit me down in Ruskin and their Commonwealth and write 'em.[5]

Unless she erred in reporting this conversation, Gilman's reference to "8 or 10 stories" making up "a book of 4 or 5000 words" suggests that she and Small had in mind vignettes even briefer than her most recent fiction, the imitations of famous authors she wrote for the *Impress* in 1894 and 1895.[6] The book they envisioned would contain stories that had yet to be written, stories that Gilman described as "carry[ing] on my work from its plane of mere argument into the popular imagina-tion."[7] At some point between November 1898 and May 1899, that plan was abandoned in favor of a reprinting of "The Yellow Wall-paper," a single story of just over 6000 words.

Gilman lectured throughout the Midwest and the South that winter, returning to Boston for three days in April 1899 and calling on Small, Maynard each day. She might at this time have agreed to the publication of "The Yellow Wall-paper" by itself, and even supplied a revised manuscript, but her diary and letters are silent about these matters. Gilman makes no mention of reading proof on the story,

5. CPS to George Houghton Gilman, 2 November 1898, Gilman Papers, Schlesinger Library. Interestingly, a volume entitled *Their Shadows Before* was published by Small, Maynard in fall 1899; the historical novel by Pauline Carrington Bouvé concerns the Turner Rebellion.

6. See Gary Scharnhorst, *Charlotte Perkins Gilman: A Bibliography* (Metuchen, N.J.: Scarecrow Press, 1985), pp. 61–63. Several of these pieces are reprinted in *The Yellow Wall-Paper and Other Stories*, ed. Robert Shulman (Oxford and New York: Oxford University Press, 1995).

7. CPS to George Houghton Gilman, 3 November 1898, Gilman Papers, Schlesinger Library; reprinted in *Journey*, p. 196.

Fig. 9. Charlotte Perkins Stetson, London, 1899. On 7 July 1899 Gilman notes in her diary "Go to Elliott & Fry's & have photograph taken—as a 'Celebrity!'" (*Diaries*, p. 784). Reprinted by permission of the Schlesinger Library, Radcliffe College.

though she had read proof the previous year when Small, Maynard published *Women and Economics*. This time, however, Gilman was out of the country in the months before the book was published. She left for England a fortnight after her visit to Boston and remained abroad until the end of August, by which time SM had already been reviewed more than a dozen times.

Gilman's publishers issued *The Yellow Wall Paper* with copyright dates of 1899, 1901, and 1911, and they wrote to Gilman on 18 September 1903 that they were awaiting "a new edition . . . from the bindery."[8] I have not located a 1903 issue, but the 1899, 1901, and 1911 issues I have examined match one another in all particulars except for the title pages. The existence of several issues, however, does not necessarily imply great demand for the book; it might only indicate fiscal caution on the part of a publisher. Small, Maynard might have printed several small batches from the same plates, rather than one large initial press run, or, more likely, the publisher simply bound the book in separate batches, using a new title page for each issue. When Gilman negotiated in 1919 to purchase the copyrights and remaining stock of her books from Small, Maynard, the deal included plates, unbound sheets (folded and gathered, ready for binding), and remaining bound copies. The delivery order in August of that year indicates that no sheets or bound copies of *The Yellow Wall Paper* remained in the publisher's inventory, though sheets and copies of *Women and Economics* and *Concerning Children* were still on hand. Surviving records do not show exactly how many copies of *The Yellow Wall Paper* were printed or sold by Small, Maynard, and the publisher was unable to supply such figures in answer to the author's inquiry at the time she bought back her books.[9] Gilman's diary records a total of $200 in advances from Small, Maynard for the four books of hers that they published, *In This Our World* (1898), *Women and Economics* (1898), *The Yellow Wall Paper* (1899), and *Concerning Children* (1900). Assuming an average advance of $50 per book, at her contracted royalty rate of 10 percent, or 5 cents per copy, *The Yellow Wall Paper* might have sold as many as a thousand copies before royalty payments commenced. Royalty statements beginning in 1902 indicate that the book sold an average of 47 copies per year between 1902 and 1914, tapering off somewhat toward the end of that period. A generous estimate, then, might put total sales of SM at 2000 copies for all issues.

When William Dean Howells anthologized "The Yellow Wall-paper" in his 1920 collection of *Great Modern American Stories* (WDH), he used *The New England Magazine* as his printer's copy, as demonstrated by both external and internal evidence. Horace Brisbin Liveright, president of the firm of Boni & Liveright, wrote to Howells regarding the acquisition of uncopyrighted selections for the collection:

"The Yellow Wallpaper" by Charlotte Perkins Stetson Gilman, from the New England magazine. I shall take steps to get this story. (Will you tell me how I can get physical possession of this story so that I will have it on hand for

---

8. Small, Maynard & Co. to CPG, 18 September 1903, Gilman Papers, Schlesinger Library, folder 134.

9. Gilman's correspondence with Small, Maynard & Co. can be found in folder 134 of the Gilman Papers, Schlesinger Library, as can the book delivery order and her surviving royalty statements.

the printer when the time comes). . . . I will also try to get a copy of the
New England Magazine.[10]

Howells's own letter to Gilman requests permission to reprint the story, but does not ask for a text of it. Replying to his request just seven months after she had purchased her copyrights back from Small, Maynard, Gilman neither offers to supply copy nor indicates a preference for the edition now belonging to her (see pages 95–96). The text that appeared in the Boni & Liveright anthology follows NE rather than SM in both accidentals and substantives. WDH corrects NE's typographical errors at 32.33, 34.13, 34.14, 39.10, 42.11, and 42.20, and regularizes NE's awkward readings at 32.7 and 34.33. Howells's text introduces a few of its own substantive changes: WDH emends a split infinitive at 31.5–6, removes extraneous words at 34.16 and 34.27–28, and regularizes a reading at 35.28, changing NE's "watch of it" to "watch for it".

Three additional texts authorized by Gilman derive ultimately from NE. The *New York Evening Post* printed "The Yellow Wall-paper" on Saturday, 21 January 1922 (pp. 9, 12), "by special arrangement with . . . the author." A boxed note demonstrates editorial awareness of all three prior editions of the story: the editors record the original publication in *The New England Magazine,* remark that "later it appeared as the title story in one of the author's books," and mention the story's appearance in Howells's anthology. NE was clearly the source for the newspaper's reprinting, for none of the substantive variants unique to SM or WDH has been reproduced, with a single exception: at 33.15, the newspaper follows SM in changing "perfect and enthusiastic" to "perfect, an enthusiastic". Accidentals show no clear pattern of derivation, but seem to follow the same sorts of conventions used two years earlier in Howells's anthology. The newspaper also presents two overlapping sets of section breaks that divide the story into sixteen sections. To break up the long columns of text visually, the paper inserts a blank line between sections and uses an enlarged capital followed by small caps for the first word or two of each new section. Sections demarcated in this way begin at 29.3, 30.7, 30.37, 31.16*, 32.29*, 33.27*, 34.37*, 35.36*, 37.5*, 38.10*, 38.20*, 39.15*, 39.28*, 40.12*, and 42.5 in the present text; the eleven sections marked with a star are also set off with a row of three spaced bullets in the blank line between sections. An additional section break at 40.27 is marked with the row of bullets but lacks the large and small capitals. With the exception of 32.29, the breaks signaled by bullets correspond to NE's original breaks. No correspondence between Gilman and the editors of the paper has been located, so there is no way to determine whether the terms of the "special arrangement" with the paper involved any authorial revision. The random placement of the added section breaks, however, suggests that the breaks were a newspaper device to enhance readability, for they do not correspond to the narrator's sessions at her diary. The *Post* text has no descendants, so far as I have been able to discover.

Carolyn Wells's 1927 reprint in the collection *American Mystery Stories* (CW) also derives from NE, though it shares many of the same grammatical and stylistic corrections made in WDH. In a few key readings—at 34.27–28 ("exhaust myself trying") and 35.27–28 ("keep watch for it")—CW matches a variant introduced in WDH, but these readings could have been arrived at independently by compositors smoothing out wordings that sounded dated by the 1920s. More tellingly, CW coincides with NE in an awkward reading at 32.7 ("an airy and comfortable room as any one need wish") even though WDH offers the more idiomatic reading, "as airy and comfortable a room as any one need wish." Additionally, CW's accidentals follow NE more often than they join WDH in departing from NE. Wells introduces one particularly noteworthy variant at 29.9: "expects that in marriage" becomes "expects that in men."

The Golden Book reprinting in October 1933 (GB) begins an important line of descent that has affected reprintings of "The Yellow Wall-paper" for six decades. It is clearly a derivative of NE transmitted through CW, for it reproduces nearly all of CW's variants, including two accidentals (36.11 and 41.5) that are found in no other texts. GB does not adopt CW's correction of NE's faulty subject-verb agreement at 34.33 ("the interminable grotesque seem to form"): GB alters this to "the interminable grotesque seems to form" although CW offers the perfectly acceptable reading of "the interminable grotesques seem to form"; this discrepancy, however, might indicate nothing more than the compositor's rejection of the unusual noun form of "grotesque." GB also fails to adopt CW's reading "expects that in men" (29.9), instead truncating the line to "expects that"—just one of more than a dozen variant wordings that GB adds to the textual history of "The Yellow Wall-paper." The editors of GB not only took liberties with the linguistic text of many passages, they also radically altered the section breaks that demarcate the narrator's sessions at her diary. GB eliminated seven of the original breaks and added five new ones, subtly affecting the way the narrator is presented. (See my Introduction, pages 8–9).

Gilman's own pen cannot be linked to these bibliographic variants in GB, even though she gave the magazine permission to publish "The Yellow Wall-paper." Rather, Gilman's story was made to conform to the editorial format that *The Golden Book* used for all its stories: the text is printed two columns per page, with an enlarged capital beginning each new section; every full page of text contains one, and only one, enlarged capital. Moreover, the capitals are spaced so that each double-page spread has the ornaments nicely balanced in opposite corners, if possible (see Fig. 10). While this design made the pages visually appealing, it also forced the editors to create extra breaks when the original text lacked one in the appropriate spot, and to delete breaks when they occurred too close to the end of a page or too near one another. That is to say, the section breaks became a design feature in GB and no

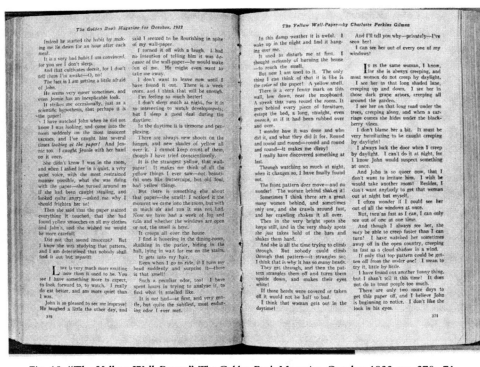

Fig. 10. "The Yellow Wall-Paper," *The Golden Book Magazine*, October 1933, pp. 370–71.

longer represented separate diary entries. Interestingly, Gilman's archive contains a clipping of GB with the text corrected in half a dozen places. Five of those six corrections insert the original breaks where they had been erroneously closed up, but none of the added section breaks is deleted.[11] Given this evidence, Gilman's involvement in or approval of GB's editorial changes seems unlikely.

Despite its lack of authority, GB stands as an important text in the publication history of "The Yellow Wall-paper." This version was reproduced in the 1930s in two anthologies aimed at college students, Cross's *A Book of the Short Story* (American Book Company, 1934), and Ferguson, Blaine, and Dumble's *Theme and Variation in the Short Story* (Cordon, 1938). Cross departs from GB in only two substantives (discussed in Notes on the Text, page 69), both of which are reproduced in Ferguson's anthology, along with two accidentals. In 1980, Ann Lane introduced GB's variants to modern readers by basing her text for *The Gilman Reader* (GR) on

11. An erroneous date of "October 1934" is inscribed in ink on the clipping's first page in what looks to be Gilman's own hand. The six corrections seem to be in pencil, and unfortunately do not reveal enough character to assess whose hand they represent (Gilman Papers, Schlesinger Library, folder 260).

The Golden Book, either directly or, more probably, by way of Ferguson's anthology.[12] GR also introduces many new accidentals, usually modernizing to conventions of punctuation prevalent in the 1980s.

After Gilman's death in 1935, "The Yellow Wall-paper" was anthologized at least fifteen times in the next thirty-seven years, bringing the number of printings to twenty-two before the Feminist Press reissued the story in a 1973 monograph edited by Elaine Hedges (FP). This edition brought Gilman's masterpiece once more before the public eye, generating a wave of interest in the work that has not yet crested. FP presents an extraordinarily faithful transcription of NE, correcting the obvious typographical errors, regularizing the hyphenation of "wall-paper," and retaining most of the punctuation of the first printing. This version introduces only one typographical error ("phospites" for "phosphites" at 29.23). It also adds two substantive variants: the omission of two sentences at 39.33–34 and the modernization of the regional phrase "go down cellar" to "go down to the cellar" at 32.5. The copyright page of FP misidentifies the text as a reprint of SM, the story's second printing. The 1996 revised edition of the Feminist Press text (FP2) corrects these errors and adds a brief Note on the Text to clarify editorial practice. Most notably, this edition returns to the inconsistent hyphenation of "wall-paper" used in NE and signals section breaks with a row of six spaced asterisks. The editor's list of emendations inadvertently omits the silent correction of typographical errors at 34.13 and 39.10. She also notes that FP2 corrects *wiil* to *will* at 34.15 in the present text (19.26 in FP2), though no such error exists in NE. Additionally, FP2 restores the hyphen in "deep-shaded" (32.10) but removes the hyphen in "old-fashioned" (32.11), and omits a comma at 32.17. Except for these minor discrepancies, FP2 presents a faithful transcription of NE.

In an unfortunate vagary of modern publishing, the respectably edited and generally accurate FP has served as the source for only half as many reprints of the story as the eccentric and nonauthoritative GR, which erroneously billed itself as a reprint of the story's first printing. (See pages 121–32 for a listing of anthologies and their sources.) This disparity suggests that editors of modern anthologies wish to offer the story to their readers in a version they believe to be closest to its original published state.

The most recent addition to the textual history of "The Yellow Wall-paper" is a volume edited by Thomas Erskine and Connie Richards for the Rutgers University Press series Women Writers: Texts and Contexts (WW). Though it claims to be an "authoritative text" of the story, WW conflates the two most important modern versions, FP and GR, without offering any rationale for the editors' choices. WW

---

12. GR follows Ferguson's text when it departs from GB and Cross: at 37.9 both GR and Ferguson change "underway" to "under way"; at 37.33 they render "O no" as "oh no"; and both omit the section break GB had inserted at 29.26–27, which falls at a page break in Cross's edition.

also introduces several new substantives (at 34.19, 37.31, and 40.4) as well as one omission (37.7). Among the accidentals, this version usually opts for more modern readings and punctuation, but not consistently so. Compare, for instance, the treatment of NE's archaic forms "to-day" (40.37), "to-morrow" (40.38 and 41.12), and "to-night" (41.12): in three instances, WW lets the hyphenated form remain, but the second time "to-morrow" appears it is altered to "tomorrow." As discussed elsewhere, WW also reduces the number of sections to six, presenting the story in half as many diary entries as it began with a century earlier.

In summarizing the publication history of "The Yellow Wall-paper," one can say that every significant version can be traced back to the story's first printing in *The New England Magazine* with no conclusive authorial intervention at any stage. NE was the direct source for Small, Maynard's 1899 monograph, William Dean Howells's 1920 anthology, the *New York Post*'s 1922 reprint, Carolyn Wells's 1927 *American Mystery Stories*, and Elaine Hedges's 1973 Feminist Press edition. The most radical departure from NE came in 1933 when *The Golden Book* introduced unauthorized readings and section breaks into a text that derived from CW. GB begat Cross (1934), which begat Ferguson (1938), which seems to have been the basis for Ann Lane's 1980 *Gilman Reader*. Through FP and GR, two quite different versions of "The Yellow Wall-paper" have circulated among critics and students during the past two decades, and those versions have recently been arbitrarily conflated by WW.

Authorial practice and preference

In light of the foregoing publication history, which text of "The Yellow Wall-paper" should an editor choose as copy-text? Would it not be best to return to Gilman's manuscript as the only known version of the story that offers demonstrable evidence of what the author really wrote? I would argue that we cannot assume that what an author wrote in manuscript and what she intended her public to read are necessarily the same thing. Each author negotiates market expectations in a different way, and editors must be cognizant of the author's attitudes toward publication and authorship itself when choosing how to present a given text.

For some authors, every stroke of the pen conveys personal nuances that the conventions of publication might flatten or obliterate. Emily Dickinson and William Blake come immediately to mind in this regard; both placed great value on individual style, even in matters of punctuation and typography. When the pressures of the literary marketplace proved too distorting for the texts they wished to present to readers, both authors chose alternatives to conventional publication: Dickinson withdrew her work from the printing-house and counting-house, while Blake took on the roles of printer, publisher, and illustrator of his own works. Extreme individuality demanded extreme measures in the face of editorial conventions and marketplace expectations. In such cases as these, an editor would be wise to stick as closely to authorial manuscripts as possible. Yet despite our predilection for a romantic view of literary production that conceives of the author as the sole originator of the creative work, not all writers insist on such authorial autonomy.

From all that can be gathered about Gilman's habits as a writer, we know she was no Dickinson or Blake. She was not a meticulous stylist, intent on conveying her personal vision with every word and comma. Her friend Alexander Black claimed that Gilman would have scoffed at any artistic theory that "implied close consciousness in writing." Her "philosophy as a literary workman," according to Black, emphasized ideas over their transmission; she rejected the belief that "the idea might be by the grace of God and the expression remain a matter of momentous individual responsibility" (page 118). Writing to her future husband, Gilman described her attitude toward literary craftsmanship: "I'm [n]o self- conscious artist. If you care little for my style why I care less—so there's no quarrel. But if I write [stories] easily and people read them widely—that's an end to be desired."[13] The sheer volume and pace of her writing after 1890 lend credence to this view of Gilman the writer. She annually turned out scores of lectures, reviews, essays, poems, and stories even before she began her one-woman journal, *The Forerunner,* for which she wrote, according to her reckoning, "21,000 w[or]ds a month" for seven years.[14]

Gilman's attitude toward spelling displays an almost triumphant disregard for convention. "I'm a wretched speller myself and always shall be, and I don't care a bit," she reported to her friend Martha Luther Lane. "There isn't one noble achievement in life that rests on spelling, so that you are understood of course. It always seemed to me a trumpery art." Admitting that "some rudiments must be acquired for the sake of other people," she joked that when she was more solvent she would send "type-written letters, spelled and punctuated by a special proof reader."[15] Far from objecting to printing-house manipulation of her texts, Gilman seems to have welcomed editorial regularization of her spelling and her often inconsistent punctuation. She was not concerned that editorial intervention would blur her artistic vision, for her focus was not on style but on content. Her aim in publishing her work seems to have been twofold: to get messages out to readers, and to get paid for those messages—promptly, if possible. This was especially true in the early 1890s, years in which Gilman struggled to establish an economic footing for herself as an author and lecturer.

There is no reason to believe that the writing and publication of her most famous

13. CPS to George Houghton Gilman, 6 November 1898, Gilman Papers, Schlesinger Library; reprinted in *Journey,* p. 198.

14. See CPG to William Dean Howells, 17 October 1919 (page 96).

15. CPS to Martha Luther Lane, 15 April 1890 and 17 June 1890. Quoted by permission of the Manuscript Collection, Rhode Island Historical Society.

story represented an exception to Gilman's usual practice. Although the possibility cannot be entirely ruled out, no immediate evidence suggests that Gilman edited or directly supervised any version of the story printed during her lifetime. The first printing, in *The New England Magazine*, seems to have taken place without Gilman's prior awareness, for she makes no mention of the story's acceptance or pending publication in her 1891 diary or in her manuscript log. It is not until June 1892 that Gilman records the story's publication; she includes it in her log in a list of items "printed and unpaid," erroneously noting the publication date as March 1892. The next two printings of the story, SM and WDH, receive passing mention in her autobiography, but again she indicates no personal intervention in those or subsequent editions. Moreover, she gave no special attention to the story that now marks her place in literary history. She relates in *The Living* that she told Howells she did not consider "The Yellow Wall-paper" to be "literature," but merely a story "with a purpose," as all her writing had a purpose; in her letter to him, she calls the story "pure propaganda" (pages 89 and 96).

The entire passage in *The Living* related to "The Yellow Wall-paper" deserves some attention, for it reveals Gilman's priorities with regard to the story at the end of her life. The bulk of her recollections concern the "tremendous impression" the work left on readers, but she devotes the first third of her account to matters of publication and payment. Scudder's rejection offends less than the agent's theft of her due remuneration for the work. Interestingly, Gilman gives a precise amount when she dismisses her loss of compensation, saying "It was only forty dollars anyway!" More probably, the magazine's payment would have been about half that amount. Editor Edwin Doak Mead reported to another contributor the previous September that "these fellows don't yet pay very much for articles—I dare say they can't afford to, as the magazine is only just now finally on its feet. For plain articles their rate has been $2.50 a page—& in illustrated articles we meet besides the cost of illustration." Mead gave Gilman the same per page figure in 1897.[16] The eight and a half text pages of "The Yellow Wall-paper" would have earned her only $21.25 by this reckoning. Yet even this smaller sum would have been exceedingly welcome to Gilman in 1892, a year she described as one of "poverty, illness, [and] heartache." Shortly after the publication of "The Yellow Wall-paper," she began running the boarding house in which she rented rooms for $20 per month. Her lectures, sermons, and occasional publications paid poorly, if at all; by the end of the year the Socialists sent one of their members "to offer assistance" to her, having heard that she was "destitute."[17] In her autobiography, she complains that she "never got a cent for

16. Edwin Doak Mead to [Albert B. Hart], 5 September 1891, Boston Public Library, Ms. 2655 (1–11). Quoted by courtesy of the Trustees of the Boston Public Library. Cf. CPS to George Houghton Gilman, 21 September 1897, Gilman Papers, Schlesinger Library; reprinted in *Journey*, p. 102.

17. See *Diaries*, pp. 507, 506.

[the story] till later publishers brought it out in book form, and very little then" (pages 87–89). Even at some distance from those years of impoverishment, Gilman focuses neither on the literary merits of the piece nor on her artistic expression of her experience. She dwells, instead, on the work the story did: the impression it made on readers, the influence it had on Mitchell's treatment of neurasthenia, and, not least, the financial work it failed to accomplish on her behalf. She concludes this episode of her reminiscences with a statement that once more emphasizes economics rather than artistry: "All these literary efforts providing but little, it was well indeed that another avenue of work opened to me at this time."

Gilman's attitudes toward literary craftsmanship in general and toward "The Yellow Wall-paper" in particular, then, suggest that the creative act probably had less significance in her frame of reference than the communicative act. This being so, an editor need not grant automatic authority to the surviving manuscript over printed versions of the story. The manuscript might disclose the author's personal inclinations for wording, spelling, or punctuation at the time it was inscribed, but it can shed no light on how the story was received—on the "impression" it made, to use Gilman's terms. That "impression" was made only after the combined efforts of editors, compositors, proofreaders, press workers, newsagents, and others had transmitted "The Yellow Wall-paper" to its first audience by way of the printed impressions on the pages of *The New England Magazine*. Gilman herself seems to have preferred this version of her text over all others. When given the opportunity to reprint the story as a monograph in 1899, she did not supply Small, Maynard & Co. with the fair copy manuscript in her possession. Nor, on the five subsequent occasions when her permission to reprint the story was sought, did Gilman indicate a preference for her manuscript over the first published edition.

The only other likely candidate for copy-text would be the Small, Maynard monograph, for it was printed by Gilman's publisher, presumably with her advance knowledge, and most of the known reviews respond to this edition. However, Gilman seems to have had no hand in the variants introduced into SM when it was derived from NE. Her own copy of SM, purported to bear annotations and marginalia in the author's own hand, is now in the possession of Denise D. Knight. I have not seen this copy as it is "not open to research," but Knight assures me that "there's nothing in the edition that should significantly change the way we read the story."[18] Even were those annotations to constitute significant revisions, they would not affect choice of copy-text, for Gilman never offered them to the reading public in a published form. Thus her private copy stands as an interesting commentary on "The Yellow Wall-paper," but does not form a pivotal part of its textual history.

The fact that SM was reviewed more widely than NE merely reminds us that

18. Private correspondence with the author, 8 August 1996.

books receive formal reviews and magazines, by and large, do not. The *Boston Transcript*'s notice of the January number of *The New England Magazine* was typical of the omnibus reviews magazines received at this time: the reviewer devotes a few sentences apiece to the major articles in the issue and then lists with minimal comment the remaining contents of "a very interesting number" (page 103). Despite the paucity of reviews, NE was probably read more widely than SM. The exact circulation of *The New England Magazine* is not known, for publishers guarded such information closely. Several issues of the magazine contain a full-page statement entitled "Why It Pays and What It Pays to Advertise in the NEW ENGLAND MAGAZINE": J. M. Potter, the journal's manager, explains that "its circulation has tripled the past year. It is constantly increasing, owing to a growing appreciation of its worth, and to the fact that it is making special efforts to extend the circulation among New Englanders in certain localities, by running special articles regarding different cities of the United States."[19] The publishers reported their circulation as 23,000 in 1892, according to *N. W. Ayer & Son's American Newspaper Annual* (Philadelphia: N. W. Ayer & Son, 1892), p. 995. Allowing for considerable editorial hyperbole, the actual circulation was at least fifteen thousand copies per issue. That is to say, *The New England Magazine* for January 1892 reached far more readers than the few thousand copies of SM that seem to have been distributed over a period of fifteen years.

Though the two approaches to textual editing that dominate today's literary scholarship often seem at odds with one another, followers of both approaches would, I believe, agree on NE as copy-text for a scholarly edition of "The Yellow Wall-paper." If it is true that a second manuscript, now lost, served as printer's copy for the story's first serial printing, an editor using the Greg-Bowers approach would argue that NE is closer to the text of the fair-copy manuscript that Gilman submitted for publication than any other witness, including AMS. McGann's followers would stress that NE was the first version of "The Yellow Wall-paper" presented to Gilman's contemporary audience for their enjoyment and criticism, by means of a mutually accepted collaboration between author and publisher. Regardless of which editorial school one belongs to, then, the choice of copy-text for an edition of "The Yellow Wall-paper" remains *The New England Magazine* of January 1892.

EDITORIAL METHODOLOGY

Presentation of text and variants

This edition presents a clear text of "The Yellow Wall-paper" followed by a complete apparatus, rather than indicating variants on the same page as the reading

---

19. *The New England Magazine*, n.s. 5, no. 6 (February 1892), p. 2 of wrappers.

text. Presenting the variants along with the reading text might imply that a process of literary construction unfolded in the successive editions, but such is not the case with this story. Though most of the variants arose after the initial magazine printing, none can be definitively (or even marginally) traced to Gilman's hand. If we allow the possibility that a manuscript other than the one surviving in Gilman's archive served as printer's copy for NE, then the few substantive variants that appeared with magazine publication might represent a different "authorial intention" than that recorded in the extant manuscript. Denise Knight's edition has made the manuscript version widely available, and readers wishing to discover how AMS differs from NE may consult the list of Pre-copy-text Substantive Variants in the present edition (pages 71–74). Any textual ambiguities among the varying printed versions can be easily recovered from the lists of variants included in the Historical Collation.

Treatment of accidentals

In the treatment of accidentals the present edition follows copy-text, emending to maintain internal consistency. Emendation has been based on the prevailing style of punctuation within NE, whenever that can be determined. All departures from copy-text are recorded in the list of Editorial Emendations (pages 70–71).

Readers should also note this edition's policies with regard to the following classes of accidentals:

Typographical inaccuracies: Obvious misspellings and incorrect punctuation have been corrected. This includes typographical errors that create nonwords, as well as inappropriate quotation marks and terminal punctuation. Frequent fragments and run-on sentences occur in the story, but they have been regarded as a feature of the narrative style and have been left unemended. Semicolon usage has also been left untouched, rather than emending to conform to modern conventions of punctuation.

Commas and dashes: Many subordinate clauses and interjections are set off by paired dashes or paired commas. In those instances where a pair is incomplete, I have added the appropriate punctuation to complete the pair. In cases where the pair is inconsistent—beginning with a dash and ending with a comma, for instance—I have chosen the punctuation that begins the sequence. When NE uses both a comma and a dash, unrelated to a paired construction, I have emended to eliminate what modern readers might perceive as a jarring redundancy, preserving only the dash. Interjections not set off by any punctuation have been emended only if it can be determined that they are typically set off elsewhere in the text. Thus commas have been inserted to set off "Besides," "Why," and "dear," since the pattern of NE's punctuation in these cases is quite clear. "Of course" shows no clear pattern, and so has been left unemended.

Hyphenation: The accidental that has received the most attention from literary critics is the hyphen in "wall-paper." Critics and editors of Gilman's story debate whether *wallpaper* should be one word, two words, or a hyphenated compound, as if the hyphen represented an artistic decision on Gilman's part. Richard Feldstein notes the inconsistent usage of the term and concludes that "from Gilman's original manuscript . . . it is apparent that the word(s) *wall(-)paper* were conceived as a shifter calculated to create ambiguity about a referent that resists analysis, even as the narrator resists her husband's diagnosis and prescription for cure."[20] In his introduction to the Oxford University Press edition of the story, Robert Shulman contends that the hyphenated spelling "emphasizes two elements, the wall or barrier, finally the bars and prison; and the paper, the surface on which is printed 'the pattern' " (p. xviii). Editor Shulman elects to retain the inconsistent usage of *The New England Magazine* "since it underscores both elements of this central symbol" (p. xxxiii).

These interpretations bear witness to the mental gymnastics of which today's critics are capable, but they have little to do with the author or any intentions she may have had. Gilman's inconsistency in this matter can be observed within her manuscript and in the course of her lifetime. The word appears with a hyphen in the manuscript title of "The Yellow Wall-Paper"; within the story, it is hyphenated six times (with two of those six being end-line hyphens) and presented as two words ("wall paper") five times. In her diary and manuscript log during this period Gilman usually treats the term as one word, "wallpaper", and she continues this usage in later discussions of the story: her typescript note, her discussion in *The Forerunner*, and her autobiography all use "wallpaper" (see pages 83–89).

Printing-house conventions demonstrate similar variability. In 1892 NE maintained the hyphen in the title and in seven of the occurrences within the story. The magazine's usage varied, however, and "wallpaper" appears in five instances. With book publication, treatment of the word first became consistent: SM separated the word as "wall paper" throughout the volume. WDH similarly rendered the term as "wall paper," while CW and GB opted for "wall-paper" throughout. Recent editors have preferred today's usage, "wallpaper," with the exceptions of Denise Knight in her edition of the manuscript and Elaine Hedges in FP2. Knight follows Gilman's manuscript usage when the word is hyphenated; however, when Gilman used "wall paper" Knight preserves the two-word reading at 33.21, 38.14, and 41.35 in the present edition but offers the one-word "wallpaper" at 31.34 and 31.38. Hedges wishes

---

20. See Feldstein, "Reader, Text, and Ambiguous Referentiality," in Golden, *CI*, p. 308.

to present the story "exactly as it appeared in its first published form" and so "preserve[s]" the inconsistencies of NE (FP2, pp. 7, 8).

Wallpaper, wall-paper, or *wall paper*? There seems little profit in cherishing either Gilman's inconsistencies or those of NE. The author's disdain for the notion of herself as a "self-conscious artist" argues against the hyphen's presence or absence representing a "calculated" decision on her part. The present edition follows the preponderance of the readings in NE by using the hyphenated form of "wall-paper," emending the copy-text to provide the consistency that Gilman and her readers would have expected. The surviving manuscript attests to her acceptance, if not consistent endorsement, of this form at the time the story was first published.

Resolutions of end-line hyphenations of compound words are listed in the apparatus section entitled "Word Division" (page 80).

Paragraphing: Paragraphing of the present edition follows NE throughout. In AMS Gilman indents the first word of each new paragraph very slightly, often less than a centimeter, making it difficult to determine paragraph breaks. In some instances, indentation is so slight that only the fact that the previous line stops well short of the righthand margin confirms the presence of a paragraph break. Gilman also had a habit of leaving large spaces before the beginning of a new sentence within a paragraph. These spaces range from about two centimeters to as much as five centimeters. Such spaces appear in NE as paragraph breaks in many but certainly not in all cases. The present edition does not rebreak the paragraphs of NE in order to follow manuscript paragraphing, for that would necessitate, in many instances, emendation of the substantives of the copy-text to a manuscript reading. Moreover, the first known review of the story remarks that it is "very paragraphic" (page 103), demonstrating that at least one member of Gilman's audience noticed the paragraphing of NE, maintained in this edition.

Readers interested in Gilman's paragraphing should consult Knight's edition of the manuscript. Knight breaks paragraphs only where there is an indentation of a first line or when the last line of a paragraph does not extend to the righthand margin. The spaces between sentences within a paragraph are not considered paragraphing signals. Knight has omitted a manuscript paragraph indentation at 30.37 in the present text, and she has added paragraph breaks at 35.39 and 37.23, as well as a blank line between paragraphs at 39.34–35.

APPARATUS

DESCRIPTION OF TEXTS

AMS   An autograph manuscript of "The Yellow Wall-paper" survives in folder
221 of the Charlotte Perkins Gilman Papers, Schlesinger Library, Radcliffe
College. The manuscript is a fair copy of 59 leaves, written in ink on ruled
wove notepaper, watermark WINDSOR MILLS, 14. 5 x 23 cm, with 21 lines per
page. The leaves are numbered 1-23, 24 ~~26~~, 24 ½ ~~27~~, 25 ~~28~~, 26 ~~29~~, 27 ~~30~~,
28–58. The upper lefthand corner of the first page is labeled in black ink
"Mrs. C. P. Stetson. Box 401 Pasadena Cal / (about 6000 words)". In red
ink on the same page there is the notation "to be returned to Mr Charles
Walter Stetson at the Fleur-de-Lys Providence R.I." Gilman used a row of
four spaced + symbols to separate the text into twelve sections, except at
35.35, where a blank line separates the sections. See pages 46–48 for a
discussion of additional manuscripts.

NE   "The Yellow Wall-Paper." *The New England Magazine*, n.s. 5 (January
1892), pp. 647–56. The text is printed in two columns, with twelve
sections separated by rows of six spaced asterisks. Three illustrations by Jo.
H. Hatfield appear on pages 647 ("I am sitting by the Window in this
Atrocious Nursery."), 651 ("She didn't know I was in the Room."), and
656 (no caption).

SM   *The Yellow Wall Paper*. Boston: Small, Maynard & Company, 1899. Pagi-
nation is <I–iv>, 1–55, <56>. Small, Maynard reissued the book in 1901
and 1911, and perhaps also in 1903, probably by making up unbound sheets
of the original printing. The 1901 and 1911 issues match the 1899 text in all
variants. The twelve sections of the text are set as chapters; each section
begins a new page and the first word of the section (two words for the
sections beginning on 34.37, 39.15, and 39.28 in the present text) is set in
large and small capitals. The section breaks at 37.4, 39.14, and 40.11 fall at
the bottom of a full page of text.

WDH   "The Yellow Wall Paper." *The Great Modern American Stories: An Anthology*.
Compiled and edited with an introduction by William Dean Howells.
New York: Boni and Liveright, 1920, pp. 320–37. Rows of eight spaced
asterisks separate the text into twelve sections.

CW   "The Yellow Wall-Paper." *American Mystery Stories*. Chosen by Carolyn
Wells. N.p.: Oxford University Press, American Branch, 1927, pp. 176–
97. Rows of nine spaced asterisks separate the text into twelve sections.

GB   "The Yellow Wall-Paper." *The Golden Book Magazine* 18 (October 1933),
pp. 363–73. The story is set in two columns and divided into ten sections,

which are separated by a blank line; the first word of each new section begins with an enlarged capital, and the remaining letters of the word (or two, for sections beginning at 36.34 and 39.31 in the present text) are set in small capitals.

FP   *The Yellow Wallpaper.* Afterword by Elaine R. Hedges. New York: The Feminist Press at The City University of New York, 1973, pp. 9–36. The copyright page identifies the text as "Reprint of the 1899 ed. published by Small, Maynard, Boston," but collation shows it to be a reprint of the 1892 *New England Magazine* version. Twelve text sections are separated by a blank line. Section breaks at 34.36 and 35.35 fall at page breaks.

GR   "The Yellow Wallpaper." *The Charlotte Perkins Gilman Reader: "The Yellow Wallpaper" and Other Fiction.* Edited and introduced by Ann J. Lane. New York: Pantheon Books, 1980, pp. 3–19. A footnote implies that the text is a reprint of the 1892 *New England Magazine* version (p. 3), but the text instead derives from *The Golden Book Magazine.* The text is divided into seven sections, each signaled by a lack of paragraph indentation and either a blank line or, when the breaks fall at the beginning of a page (31.15 and 40.26), a row of five spaced type ornaments.

WW   *The Yellow Wallpaper.* Edited and with an introduction by Thomas L. Erskine and Connie L. Richards. Women Writers: Texts and Contexts Series. New Brunswick: Rutgers University Press, 1993, pp. 29–50. A footnote identifies the text as "From *New England Magazine*, January 1892" (p. 29). The text's six sections are signaled by a blank line with no indentation of the first paragraph.

NOTES ON THE TEXT

29.26–27   The section break that GB inserts here falls at a page break in Cross's edition (1934). It is not included in Ferguson (1938) or GR.

31.32   In AMS Gilman originally referred to the baby as "her", but emended to "him".

32.37   blank walls] Cross's edition misprints this as "black walls", a reading repeated in Ferguson (1938).

38.19   The section break falls at a page break in WW. No blank lines are visible, suggesting that WW here followed GR in omitting the break.

42.8   GB's insertion of "Jenny" is regularized to "Jennie" in Cross (1934), as well as in Ferguson (1938) and GR.

42.20   The manuscript reading "Jane!" appeared in NE as "Jane?" This has prompted many editorial emendations and commentaries over the years. The texts collated here emend only the punctuation, changing the question mark to a period or an exclamation point. However, as early as 1937 editors of anthologies began changing "Jane" to "Jennie" (see the Appendix, pp. 121–32). "Jane" and "Jennie" are both forms of the feminized version of the Hebrew "John," and "Jennie" was a common nineteenth-century diminutive of "Jane." Thus there seems no reason to reject "Jane" as a possible reading, referring to John's sister.

Editorial Emendations

This list records all emendations of the copy-text made in the present edition. Adopted readings are at the left; rejected readings are at the right. For each accepted reading, the earliest source in which it appears is identified by a symbol; the Historical Collation offers a full history of the readings in the editions collated. Where no symbol appears after an accepted reading, all texts other than the rejected NE agree with the reading of the present text.

	Emended text		NE
29.14	mind)—*perhaps*		mind—) *perhaps*
29.23	it is—and	WDH	it is, and
30.26	hangings! But	WDH	hangings! but
31.9	repellent	WDH	repellant
31.14	away—he	AMS	away,—he
31.29	able—to	SM	able,—to
32.7	is as airy	AMS	is an airy
32.7	comfortable a room	AMS	comfortable room
32.33	breadths	AMS	breaths
33.10	bed, which	SM	bed which
33.12	But		"But
33.21	wall-paper	GB	wallpaper
34.9	wall-paper	AMS	wallpaper
34.10	wall-paper	AMS	wallpaper
34.13	It is		It it
34.14	not been	SM	nos been
34.33	all—the	GB	all,—the
34.33	grotesques	AMS	grotesque
35.21	wall-paper	AMS	wallpaper
35.27	wise—but	WDH	wise,—but
36.4	wall-paper	AMS	wallpaper
36.26	Really, dear, you	AMS	Really dear you

37.24	pattern, I mean, SM	pattern I mean,
37.32	habit, I am convinced, SM	habit I am convinced,
37.36	hypothesis, that SM	hypothesis,—that
39.1	at first—and GR	at first, and
39.10	furniture	furnitnre
40.27	John had to AMS	John to
40.29	thing!—but AMS	thing! but
41.5	me—not AMS	me,—not
41.31	Besides, I SM	Besides I
42.5	Why, there's SM	Why there's
42.10	John, dear! SM	John dear!
42.11	plantain	plaintain
42.13	indeed—"Open AMS	indeed, "Open
42.20	Jane! AMS	Jane?

PRE-COPY-TEXT SUBSTANTIVE VARIANTS

The following list records all substantive differences between the surviving manuscript of "The Yellow Wall-paper" and the first printing in *The New England Magazine* of January 1892. I have not listed accidentals since Gilman's usage was often inconsistent and her attitude toward her printed works suggests that she did not consider matters of punctuation to be of great importance. (See my discussion on pages 60–61.) I have, however, included instances in which Gilman underscored words in her manuscript, but the compositors of *The New England Magazine* set the words in roman type instead of italics. Page and line numbers refer to the present text. Manuscript readings that have been adopted in the present text are marked by a star preceding the page and line number. The notes to Denise Knight's edition of the manuscript record sixteen variants "which seem particularly noteworthy" (p. 223); these are marked with a dagger (†). Knight's edition mistranscribes the manuscript in the following instances: 29.7, "still I would" should be "still I will"; 30.26, "windows" should be "window"; 32.27, "*mustn't*" should be "mustn't"; 35.33–34, "take me from here" should be "take me away from here"; 37.36, "as scientific hypothesis" should be "as a scientific hypothesis"; and 41.29–30, "out the window" should be "out of the window".

	NE	**AMS**
†29.3	myself	I
29.7	something	something
29.13	would not	wouldn't
30.2	meet with heavy	meet heavy
30.5	feel bad.	feel badly.

†30.6	talk about	write about
30.7	road, quite	road, and quite
†30.16	the place has	it has
30.16	for years.	for years and years.
30.17	is	<u>is</u>
30.19	moonlight	moonlit
30.27	would not	wouldn't
30.30	loving, and hardly	loving, hardly
†30.31	takes all care from me,	takes every care,
30.32	and so I feel	and I feel
30.38	sunshine	sunlight
30.41	boys' school	boy's school
31.10	sunlight.	sun.
31.23	does not	doesn't
31.25	nervousness.	nervous.
31.32	*cannot*	can <u>not</u>
31.33	never was nervous	was never nervous
32.7	It is	It <u>is</u>
★32.7	is an airy	is as airy
★32.7	comfortable room	comfortable a room
32.7–8	would not	wouldn't
32.12–13	wharf belonging to	wharf that belongs to
32.20	press of ideas	pressure of ideas
32.27	must not	<u>mustn't</u>
★32.33	breaths	breadths
†32.36	they have	~~they~~ inanimate things have
33.5	wonder! I	wonder! for I
33.13	must not	mustn't
33.15	perfect and	perfect—, an
33.23	where the sun	when the sun
33.31	thing	<u>thing</u>
34.12	it is	it's
★34.13	It it	It is
34.14	has nos	hasn't
34.17	principle	principles
34.20	breadths	breadth
34.22	"debased Romanesque"	debased Romanesque
†34.29	frieze	border
34.32	upon it	on it
★34.33	grotesque	grotesques
35.4	am awfully lazy	am lazy, awfully lazy

†35.14	his arms	his strong arms
35.20	one	<u>one</u>
†35.22	If we	If I
35.32	it is	it's
35.39	all around	all round
†36.4	till I felt creepy.	till it made me creepy.
36.15	cannot	can't
36.28	body	<u>body</u>
36.30	and for our	and our
36.31	that idea	<u>that</u> idea
36.34	we went	he went
37.1	wasn't, and lay	wasn't. I lay
37.2	that front	the front
37.5	On a pattern	In a pattern
†37.5	a lack	a certain lack
37.9	following, it	following it, it
37.11	upon you	on you
37.15	sometimes!	<u>sometimes!</u>
37.24	bars	<u>bars</u>
37.24–25	behind it is	behind is
37.26	that dim	the dim
37.29	me	<u>me</u>
37.33	them	<u>them</u>
37.37	did not	didn't
38.7	I know	<u>I</u> know
38.10–11	something more to	something to
†38.11–12	more quiet	much more quiet
38.16	even want to take	even take
38.24	cannot	can <u>not</u>
38.25	that wall-paper	that paper
†38.25	wall-paper! It	paper. A sickly penetrating suggestive yellow. It
†38.28	is something else about	is another thing about
38.32	creeps	creep
39.10	runs round	runs all round
★39.10	furnitnre	furniture
39.20	in the very shady	in very shady
39.37	humiliating	unpleasant
40.5	myself.	me.
40.7	one at one	one at a
†40.12	try it	try tearing it

★40.27	John to	John had to
40.28	until	till
41.9	servants are gone,	servants,
41.9	things are gone,	things,
41.18	till	until
41.22	could not	couldn't
41.23	This bed	The bed
41.24	lift and push	lift or push
41.24	until	till
41.31	it. Of course not.	it of course!
41.35	come	came
†42.9	break down that	break that
†42.9	beautiful door	beautiful strong door
★42.11	plaintain	plantain
42.14	front door	front steps
42.15	slowly, and said	slowly. I said
★42.20	Jane?	Jane!
†42.23	him every time!	him!

HISTORICAL COLLATION

The texts represented in the following table have been selected for their relevance to the story's transmission. I have included all but two versions of the story printed during CPG's lifetime. A version derived from NE, with corrections of obvious printer's errors, was reprinted with Gilman's permission by the *New York Evening Post* on 21 January 1922. Gilman also gave permission to E. A. Cross to reprint the story in his 1934 anthology *A Book of the Short Story* (see page 102); Cross's text exactly matches GB, except as indicated in the Notes on the Text (page 69).

The collation also includes three modern texts. The 1973 Feminist Press edition, edited by Elaine R. Hedges, and the 1980 *Gilman Reader*, edited by Ann J. Lane, are the versions of "The Yellow Wall-paper" best known to modern readers, for they have been the source of most reprintings of the story in the past two decades. The recent volume in Rutgers University Press's series Women Writers: Texts and Contexts, edited by Thomas L. Erskine and Connie L. Richards, offers itself as "the authoritative text" of the story, and is included here so readers can ascertain how it compares with other versions. An Appendix (pages 121–32) lists more than one hundred printings and reprintings of "The Yellow Wall-paper," noting the textual sources and significant variants found in anthologies, including many of the most popular textbooks used in college classrooms today.

The following list records all substantives and accidentals that appear in the collated texts subsequent to the 1892 *New England Magazine,* the copy-text for the present edition. The reading in the present edition appears to the left of the bracket; the variant reading and its source(s) appear to the right of the bracket. Any unlisted texts may be presumed to agree with the reading in the present text. For cases in which the present edition departs from the copy-text, the source of the emended reading can be found in the list of Editorial Emendations (pages 70–71). Discrepancies between Gilman's autograph manuscript and the copy-text are noted separately in the list of Pre-copy-text Substantive Variants (pages 71–74).

29.1	Wall-paper] WALL-PAPER NE; WALL PAPER SM, WDH; Wall-Paper GB; Wallpaper FP, WW; WALLPAPER GR
29.5	house, and] house and GR
29.6	felicity—but] felicity,—but SM
29.9	expects that in marriage.] expects that in men. CW; expects that. GB, GR
29.14	mind)—] mind—) NE
29.16	You see he] You see, he SM, WDH, GR, WW
29.16–17	sick! ¶ And] sick! And WDH, CW, GB, GR
29.20	depression—a] depression,—a SM
29.20	tendency—what] tendency,—what SM
29.23	phosphites] phospites FP
29.23	phosphites—whichever] phosphites,—whichever SM
29.23	it is—and] it is, and NE, FP; it is,—and SM
29.23–24	and journeys, and air, and exercise,] and air and exercise, and journeys, GB, GR
29.26	Personally, I] Personally I SM
29.26–27	ideas. ¶ Personally,] ideas. § Personally, GB
29.27	Personally, I] Personally I SM
30.3	condition if] condition, if GR
30.14	greenhouses, too, but] greenhouses, but GB, GR
30.15	co-heirs] coheirs FP, WW
30.16	anyhow, the] anyhow the GB
30.17	afraid, but] afraid; but SM
30.19	*draught*] draught WDH, CW, GB, GR
30.23	so, I] so I SM, WDH, CW, GB, GR
30.24	myself—before] myself,—before SM
30.24	at least, and] at least,—and SM; at least—and WDH
30.25	opened on the] opened onto the GR
30.26	hangings! But] hangings! but NE, SM, FP
30.33	we came here] he came here GB, GR
30.36	nursery at] nursery, at SM

30.38	first and] first, and GB, GR
30.38	playroom] playground SM
30.39	judge; for] judge, for GR
31.3–4	life. ¶ One] life. One GR
31.4	sprawling flamboyant] sprawling, flamboyant GB, GR, WW
31.5–6	enough to constantly] enough constantly to WDH, CW, GB, GR
31.6	irritate and] irritate, and SM
31.6	lame uncertain] lame, uncertain SM
31.8	unheard of] unheard-of SM, WDH, GR, WW
31.9	repellent] repellant NE, SM, GB
31.9	revolting; a] revolting: a GR, WW
31.9	smouldering] smoldering CW
31.9	smouldering unclean] smouldering, unclean SM
31.10–11	sunlight. ¶ It] sunlight. It GR
31.14	away—he] away,—he NE, SM, FP
31.23	no *reason*] no reason GR
31.29	able—to] able,—to NE, FP
31.34, 31.38, 33.7, 38.14, 38.16, 38.25, 41.35	
	wall-paper] wall paper SM, WDH; wallpaper GR, WW
31.35	afterwards] afterward GB, GR
31.36	than to] that to WDH
32.3	I said, "there] I said. "There GR, WW
32.5	go down cellar] go down to the cellar FP, WW
32.5	cellar, if] cellar if SM
32.7	as airy and] an airy and NE, CW, GB, FP
32.7	comfortable a room] comfortable room NE, CW, GB, FP
32.7	any one] anyone GR, WW
32.10	garden, those] garden—those GR
32.10	deep-shaded] deepshaded FP
32.16	story-making, a] story-making a SM
32.23	well, John] well John SM
32.24	fireworks] fire-works SM
32.24	pillow-case] pillowcase CW
32.30	upside down] upside-down SM
32.31	I get] I got SM
32.32	crawl, and] crawl and GB
32.32	absurd, unblinking] absurd unblinking GR
32.33	breadths] breaths NE, FP
32.39	big, old] big old SM, GR
33.10	bed, which] bed which NE, CW, GB, FP
33.12	But] "But NE

33.15   perfect and enthusiastic] perfect, an enthusiastic   SM
33.17–18   windows. ¶ There] windows. § There   GB
33.18   lovely shaded winding] lovely, shaded, winding   SM
33.21, 34.9, 34.10, 35.21, 36.4
                  wall-paper] wallpaper   NE, GR;   wall paper   SM, WDH
33.23   faded and] faded, and   SM
33.23   so—I] so, I   SM
33.24   figure, that] figure that   GR
33.24   skulk] sulk   SM
33.28   gone and] gone, and   GR, WW
33.29   mother] Mother   GR, WW
34.1   worth while] worthwhile   GR, WW
34.13   It is as good] It it as good   NE
34.14   has not been] has nos been   NE
34.16   of a conclusion.] of conclusion.   WDH
34.17   principle] principles   SM
34.19   I ever] I have ever   WW
34.21   one way each] one way, each   SM, GR
34.21   alone, the] alone; the   GR
34.22   *delirium tremens*] delirium tremens   WDH, CW, GB, GR
34.25   sea-weeds] seaweeds   SM, FP, WW
34.27–28   myself in trying] myself trying   WDH, CW, GB, GR, WW
34.29   horizontal] horizonal   GB
34.32   crosslights] cross-lights   SM, WDH
34.32–33   radiation after] radiation, after   SM
34.33   all—the] all,—the   NE, SM, WDH, CW, FP
34.33   grotesques] grotesque   NE, GB, GR
34.33   seem] seems   GB, GR
34.33   centre] center   GR, WW
34.35   nap I] nap, I   SM, WDH, GR
34.35–37   guess. § I] guess. ¶ I   GB, GR, WW
35.3–4   relief. ¶ Half] relief. § Half   GB, GR, WW
35.4–5   much. ¶ John] much. John   GB, GR
35.5   cod liver] cod-liver   SM
35.8   wish] wished   SM
35.12–13   weakness I] weakness, I   SM, WDH, GR
35.15   it tired] he tired   SM
35.19   any silly] my silly   SM
35.20   comfort, the] comfort—the   GR
35.22   used it, that] used it that   SM
35.25   here after] here, after   SM, WDH

35.25	after all, I] after all. I SM, WDH; after all; I GR
35.27	more—I] more,—I SM
35.27	wise—but] wise,—but NE, SM, FP
35.28	watch of it] watch for it WDH, CW, GB, GR
35.29	that paper] that wall-paper GB; that wallpaper GR, WW
35.29	knows but me] knows about but me GB, GR
35.34–36	here! § It] here! ¶ It GB, GR, WW
35.39	around just] around, just SM
36.11	talk, so] talk so CW, GB
36.13	said he, "our] said he. "Our GR
36.15–16	Of course if] Of course, if GR
36.16	danger, I] danger I SM
36.18	better, I] better. I SM, WDH
36.20	evening when] evening, when SM
36.20	here, but] here but GR
36.20	morning when] morning, when SM
36.20	away!] away. SM
36.21	hug, "she] hug; "she SM; hug. "She GR
36.21	pleases!] pleases. SM
36.23	morning!] morning. SM
36.26	Really, dear, you] Really dear you NE, FP
36.28	body perhaps] body, perhaps SM
36.28	perhaps—"] perhaps"— SM
36.33–34	so?" ¶ So] so?" § So GB
37.1	wasn't, and lay] wasn't,—I lay SM
37.3–5	separately. § On] separately. ¶ On GB, GR, WW
37.7	unreliable enough, and infuriating enough, but] unreliable enough, but WW
37.9	underway] under way SM, WDH, GR
37.10	back-somersault and] back somersault, and SM; back somersault and WDH
37.14	convolutions—why] convolutions,—why SM
37.18–19	first long] first, long WDH, CW, GB
37.23	candlelight] candle light FP, WW
37.24	pattern, I] pattern I NE, WDH, CW, GB, FP
37.26	behind, that] behind,—that SM
37.27	sub-pattern, but] sub-pattern,—but SM
37.31	Indeed he] Indeed, he SM, WDH
37.31	habit by making] habit of making WW
37.32	habit, I] habit I NE, CW, GB, FP
37.32	for you see I] for, you see, I SM, WDH; for you see, I GR

37.33	awake—] awake,— SM	
37.33	O no!] oh, no! SM, GR, WW; O, no! WDH, GB; Oh, no! CW	
37.34	fact is I] fact is, I SM, WDH	
37.36	hypothesis, that] hypothesis,—that NE, FP; hypothesis—that WW	
37.36	paper!] paper. WW	
37.40	room, and] room and WW	
38.2	paper—she] paper she SM; paper, she GR	
38.5	John's, and] John's and GR	
38.8	myself!] myself. WW	
38.10	see I] see, I GR	
38.18–20	enough. § I'm] enough. ¶ I'm GB, GR, WW	
38.20	feeling ever so much] feeling so much GB, GR	
38.20	better! I] better! ¶ I GB, GR	
38.21	in the daytime] during the daytime GB	
38.26	old foul] old, foul GR, WW	
38.30	rain, and] rain and GB	
38.30	not,] not SM	
39.1	at first—and] at first, and NE, SM, WDH, CW, GB, FP	
39.3	awful, I] awful. I SM, GB, GR	
39.8	paper! A] paper—a SM	
39.8	smell.] smell! SM	
39.10	runs round] runs around SM	
39.10	furniture] furnitnre NE	
39.13–15	dizzy! § I] dizzy! ¶ I GB, GR, WW	
39.24–25	upside down] upside-down SM	
39.26–28	bad. § I] bad. ¶ I GB, WW	
39.30–31	windows! ¶ It] windows! § It GB	
39.33–34	I see her in that long . . . the garden.] {omitted} FP	
40.3	queer now, that] queer, now, that SM; queer now that GR	
40.4	get that woman] let that woman WW	
40.8	her, she] her she SM	
40.8–9	turn! ¶ I] turn! I GB, GR	
40.10	a high wind.] a wind. GB, GR	
40.10–12	wind. § If] wind. ¶ If GB, GR, WW	
40.25	are secretly affected] are affected GB, GR	
40.27	John had to stay] John to stay NE, WDH, CW, FP; John is to stay SM, GB, GR, WW	
40.29	thing!—but] thing! but NE, SM, WDH, CW, FP; thing; but GB, GR; thing! But WW	
40.31	moonlight and] moonlight, and SM	
40.33	she shook, I shook] she shook. I shook GR	

40.36	at me, I] at me I SM
40.37	to-day] today GB, GR
40.38	to-morrow] tomorrow GB, GR
41.1	amazement] amazment GB
41.5	me—not] me,—not NE, FP; Me—not CW, GB, GR
41.7–8	could; and] could, and GR, WW
41.12	to-night] tonight GB, GR
41.12	to-morrow] tomorrow GB, GR, WW
41.31	Besides, I] Besides I NE, WDH, CW, GB, FP, GR, WW
41.35	wall-paper as] wall paper, as SM
42.5	Why, there's] Why there's NE, CW, GB, FP, WW
42.8	crying for] crying to Jenny for GB; crying to Jennie for GR, WW
42.10	John, dear!] John dear! NE, CW, FP, GR, WW
42.10	voice, "the] voice. "The GR
42.11	plantain] plaintain NE
42.13	said—very] said, very WDH, CW, GB, GR, WW
42.13	indeed—"Open] indeed, "Open NE, SM, WDH, CW, GB, FP, GR, WW
42.14	door under] door, under SM
42.14–15	leaf!" ¶ And then] leaf!" And then GB, GR
42.16	it of] it, of SM
42.18	doing!] doing? SM
42.20	Jane!] Jane? NE; Jane. WDH, CW, GB, FP, GR, WW

Word Division

The following list records the forms used in the present edition for compound words hyphenated at line-ends in the copy-text (NE). All of the compounds adopt the form used in AMS, with these exceptions: "sub-pattern" (33.21) appears hyphenated elsewhere in NE; "wall- paper" (38.25) follows the editorial policy described on pages 66–67; and "moonlight" (40.31) breaks at a line-end in AMS, but is treated as an unhyphenated compound elsewhere in AMS and NE. No compounds or possible compounds are broken at line ends in the present edition.

30.15 co-heirs
33.15 housekeeper
33.21 sub-pattern
34.25 sea-weeds
38.25 wall-paper
39.36 blackberry
40.31 moonlight

Documents of the Case

[The documents are divided into four sections and are arranged chronologically within each section. The author's own remarks concerning "The Yellow Wall-paper" are followed by a selection of letters to and from Gilman, spanning the period from the month the story was written until a year before her death. The third section reprints twenty-six reviews or excerpts of reviews that appraise the story as it appeared in 1892, 1899, 1920, and 1927; these range from full-page analyses of "The Yellow Wall-paper" to brief mentions of it as a part of larger collections. The selection of documents ends with excerpts from longer essays that are not primarily reviews of "The Yellow Wall-paper" but that nevertheless shed light on the story's publication and reception, or on Gilman's working methods. Each document is preceded by a heading that indicates its source as fully as possible; many of the reviews are known only from clippings on which the source notes are sometimes illegible or incomplete. In editorial notes before and after the individual documents I have provided contextual information and identified important persons or events. All original spellings are preserved and omissions within documents are marked with ellipses. Editorial square brackets are used only to add explanatory information or missing punctuation.]

GILMAN'S REMARKS ON THE STORY

[Because "The Yellow Wall-paper" had lasting appeal, Gilman had frequent occasion to comment upon it. As her diaries reveal, she read the story aloud to small audiences before it was published and continued to do so periodically until at least 1899. Gilman often minimized its value as literature, and she diminished its importance in comparison with her other works. In 1919 she tried to buy back the rights to The Yellow Wall Paper, Women and Economics, In This Our World, and Concerning Children from Small, Maynard & Co.; writing to her

publisher she referred to those works as "the 'three-and-a-bit' of my books which [you] publish."[1] Despite such deprecations, she did count "The Yellow Wall-paper" among her important works. Asked to supply data on herself for a history of sociology, she included the story among her list of publications, referring to it as a "psychopathological study."[2] She told and retold the story of its publication and reception in several forms. Reprinted here are an undated typescript account, as well as the versions of the story's history published by Gilman in her magazine The Forerunner (1913) and in her autobiography, The Living of Charlotte Perkins Gilman (1935). See also the account given to W. D. Howells in the letter of 17 October 1919 (page 96).]

DIARIES AND MANUSCRIPT LOG

[The extant diaries span the period from 1 January 1876, when Charlotte Anna Perkins was just fifteen, until 3 May 1903, when Charlotte Perkins Gilman was an internationally known lecturer and writer. Now a part of the Charlotte Perkins Gilman Papers, owned by the Schlesinger Library on the History of Women in America at Radcliffe College, the diaries have been published in a two-volume set edited by Denise D. Knight. The diaries largely chronicle the quotidian facts of the writer's daily life, including chores, visits, correspondence, expenses, and income. There are several gaps in the sequence, most notably the break after 19 April 1887, when Gilman began her treatment at Dr. S. Weir Mitchell's sanitarium. Gilman resumed her diary at the beginning of 1890, just when the pace and quality of her writing escalated. In addition to her diary, Gilman also kept a manuscript log between 1 March 1890 and 23 August 1892. Here she recorded the poems, essays, and stories she sent to various magazines, along with their eventual publication dates and, occasionally, the rate of payment she received. Along with many of Gilman's notebooks and journals, the manuscript log remains unpublished. It can be found in box XXVII, volume 23, of the Gilman Papers at the Schlesinger Library.

The following excerpts from these two sorts of records present information relevant to the publication and reception history of "The Yellow Wall-paper." I have included diary and log entries related to other works if they concern The New England Magazine, W. D. Howells, or the literary agency of Henry Austin. I have also included Gilman's references to reading the story aloud to various friends or family members. She seems to have kept a copy of the manuscript for such readings, even as a fair copy was circulating among editors and journals. Entries from the diary and manuscript log are presented together in a single chronological sequence; the source of each entry is identified as "Diary" or "Log."]

11 March 1890 [Log]   "The Giant Wistaria" to N.E. Mag. via Walter

---

1. CPG to Norman White, 17 January 1919, Gilman Papers, Schlesinger Library.
2. CPG to L. L. Bernard, 16 September 1927, Gilman Papers, Schlesinger Library.

14 June 1890 [Log]   "The Yellow Wall-paper" <u>Scribner</u>
[This entry is crossed out, as seems to have been her habit when a magazine rejected a submission.]

16 June 1890 [Diary]   Letter from W. D. Howells praising "Similar Cases" and ["]Women of Today".

24 August 1890 [Diary]   Work hard & achieve nothing! A walk with Kate towards night. Finish copy of Yellow Wallpaper in the evening.

27 August 1890 [Log]   "The Yellow Wallpaper" to Wm. D. Howells

28 August 1890 [Diary]   Send "Yellow Wallpaper" to Howells.

23 September 1890 [Diary]   Letter from Mr. Henry Austin, "Traveller Literary Syndicate". Copy and arrange mss. to send him.

27 September 1890 [Diary]   Write letters and send off all ~~last~~ this week's mss. to Mr. Austin.

27 September 1890 [Log]   (To Henry Austin—"Traveller Literary Syndicate.")

    1   "A Joke Reversed."
    2   "Are Women ~~Normal?~~ Better Than Men?"
    3   "Society and The Philosopher"
    4   "The Son of Both" (poem)
    5   "A Xmas Carol for Los Angeles" (poem)
    6   "A Conservative" (poem)
    7   "Another Conservative" (poem)
    8   "The Survival of the Fittest." [(]poem)
    9   "Ideas". (poem)
    10 "Song" (poem)
    11 "The Prophets.["] [(]poem)

[According to her manuscript log, Gilman sent "Society and The Philosopher" and "Are Women Better Than Men?" to <u>Kate Fields' Washington</u> in mid-November; a month later she sent "Are Women Better Than Men?" and "Another Conservative" to <u>The Pacific Monthly</u>; and in mid-January 1891 she offered "A Conservative" to <u>Life</u> and "The Survival of the Fittest" to <u>The New Nation</u>. The pieces were eventually published in the journals to which Gilman herself submitted them.]

26 October 1890 [Diary]   Copy & send off all Mer-Songs etc. to E. E. Hale. Also send "Yellow Wallpaper" to Mr. Austin. Very tired & weak.

26 October 1890 [Log]   "The Yellow Wallpaper" Mr. Henry Austin (Trav. Lit. Syn.)
[The prior log entry records ten children's pieces about mer-people sent "To Uncle Edward (Traveller Literary Syndicate)." A later notation indicates that those same ten were "bought by Walter for $100.00."]

14 February 1891 [Diary]   Mr. Henry Austin sent me his book—"Vagabond Verses".

25 February 1891 [Diary]   Miss Knight comes over to my house and gets me to send her a doctor for her heart trouble—as she does not like to alarm the boarding house. Nellie and I come over, and I read to them "The Unexpected" and "The Yellow Wallpaper."
[This is the first of several readings of "The Yellow Wall-paper" that Gilman records in her diary after having sent a copy of the story to Henry Austin.]

20 March 1891 [Diary]   Father calls. A Mr. Simeon Stetson calls. Other people call, lots of 'em. Go to Dr. Charlotte Brown's in the afternoon. Meet Mrs. Dunton there, sister of Mrs. Howe of L.A. . . . Read "Yellow Wall Paper" to the family in the evening.

22 April 1891 [Diary]   I am also to read ghost stories tonight at Mrs. Atherton's. . . . The ghosts were a failure, but the party was jolly. . . .

23 April 1891 [Diary]   A good night's rest—what there was of it! Breakfast in bed. Read The Yellow Wallpaper to Mrs. Atherton. She likes it.
[Gilman apparently did not read "The Yellow Wall-paper" as one of the "ghost stories" of the previous evening.]

13 January 1892 [Diary]   Call on Mrs. McChesney & leave N. E. Mag.
[Though she makes no mention of her story, this entry suggests that Gilman saw the January 1892 issue of <u>The New England Magazine</u> in which "The Yellow Wall-paper" first appeared.]

21 January 1892 [Diary]   Write "The Amoeboid Cell". . . . Send <u>Cell</u> and <u>Cart before the horse</u> to Howells.

18 February 1892 [Diary]   Write to Mrs Carter (England) and send her Yellow Wallpaper

30 December 1898 [Diary]   Go to Mary Smith's to dinner, read "Yellow Wallpaper" and recite variously. Good time.

28 May 1899 [Diary]   The Normans very cordial and nice. . . . Read them <u>The Yellow Wall-paper</u>—they advise about placing my things here [England].
[The Small, Maynard & Co. monograph edition of the story was published the following month. Gilman received copies of the book while still in England in August 1899.]

Typescript, "The Yellow Wall Paper— Its History & reception"

Gilman Papers, Schlesinger Library, folder 221.

[A handwritten heading signed "KBSC," the initials of Gilman's daughter Katharine Beecher Stetson Chamberlin, identifies the document as "The Yellow Wall Paper—Its History & reception—Note left by C.P.G." The note is undated, but the reference to "college rhetoric courses" may have arisen from Gilman's correspondence with Edith Foster Flint in 1923 (see page 97).]

"<u>The Yellow Wallpaper</u>" was written in two days, with the thermometer at one hundred and three—in Pasadena, Cal.

It was put in the hands of an agent, and offered to The Atlantic Monthly. Mr. Horace P. Scudder, then the editor, declined it in these terms: ~~My dear Mrs Stetson~~ "I am returning herewith the manuscript of "<u>The Yellow Wallpaper</u>". I should never forgive myself if I made other people as miserable as reading your story has made me."

A Boston physician wrote a protest to The Transcript, asserting that such a story should not be allowed to appear in print—that it was "enough to drive people mad to read it".

A ~~Kansas~~ Western physician, one Dr. Bromwell Jones, wrote to the author that the story was "the best study of incipient insanity I have ever seen, and, begging your pardon, have you been there ?"

The story ~~It is~~ well known among alienists, and in one case caused an eminent specialist in that field to state that he had changed his treatment of neurasthenia since reading it.

In some cases it is used in college in rhetoric courses.

Following its first publication, a man wrote to inquire if it was founded on fact. He knew of a woman, similarly affected, and treated in the same mistaken manner by her friends. When satisfied as to the basis of the story, he gave it to these friends to read, and it so alarmed them that they forthwith altered their methods and the woman got well.

"Why I Wrote The Yellow Wallpaper?"

The Forerunner 4 (October 1913), p. 271.

Many and many a reader has asked that. When the story first came out, in the *New England Magazine* about 1891, a Boston physician made protest in *The Transcript*. Such a story ought not to be written, he said; it was enough to drive anyone mad to read it.

Another physician, in Kansas I think, wrote to say that it was the best description of incipient insanity he had ever seen, and—begging my pardon—had I been there?

Now the story of the story is this:

For many years I suffered from a severe and continuous nervous breakdown tending to melancholia—and beyond. During about the third year of this trouble I went, in devout faith and some faint stir of hope, to a noted specialist in nervous diseases, the best known in the country. This wise man put me to bed and applied the rest cure, to which a still good physique responded so promptly that he concluded there was nothing much the matter with me, and sent me home with solemn advice to "live as domestic a life as far as possible," to "have but two hours' intellectual life a day," and "never to touch pen, brush or pencil again as long as I lived." This was in 1887.

I went home and obeyed those directions for some three months, and came so near the border line of utter mental ruin that I could see over.

Then, using the remnants of intelligence that remained, and helped by a wise friend, I cast the noted specialist's advice to the winds and went to work again—work, the normal life of every human being; work, in which is joy and growth and service, without which one is a pauper and a parasite; ultimately recovering some measure of power.

Being naturally moved to rejoicing by this narrow escape, I wrote *The Yellow Wallpaper*, with its embellishments and additions to carry out the ideal (I never had hallucinations or objections to my mural decorations) and sent a copy to the physician who so nearly drove me mad. He never acknowledged it.

The little book is valued by alienists and as a good specimen of one kind of literature. It has to my knowledge saved one woman from a similar fate—so terrifying her family that they let her out into normal activity and she recovered.

But the best result is this. Many years later I was told that the great specialist had admitted to friends of his that he had altered his treatment of neurasthenia since reading *The Yellow Wallpaper*.

It was not intended to drive people crazy, but to save people from being driven crazy, and it worked.

EXCERPT FROM *THE LIVING OF CHARLOTTE PERKINS GILMAN:*
AN AUTOBIOGRAPHY

New York: D. Appleton-Century, 1935), pp. 118–21.

[In this account, Gilman refers to several pieces of correspondence, some of which are extant.
Complete texts of the letters from Scudder, M. D., and Dr. Brummell Jones, and Gilman's
letter to W. D. Howells can be found on pages 91, 103, 93, and 96 in the present
text.]

Besides "Similar Cases" the most outstanding piece of work of 1890 was "The
Yellow Wallpaper." It is a description of a case of nervous breakdown beginning
something as mine did, and treated as Dr. S. Weir Mitchell treated me with what I
considered the inevitable result, progressive insanity.

This I sent to Mr. Howells, and he tried to have the *Atlantic Monthly* print it, but
Mr. Scudder, then the editor, sent it back with this brief card:

> DEAR MADAM,
>   Mr. Howells has handed me this story.
>   I could not forgive myself if I made others as miserable as I have
> made myself!
>   Sincerely yours,
>   H.E. SCUDDER.

This was funny. The story was meant to be dreadful, and succeeded. I suppose he
would have sent back one of Poe's on the same ground. Later I put it in the hands of
an agent who had written me, one Henry Austin, and he placed it with the *New*
England Magazine. Time passed, much time, and at length I wrote to the editor of
that periodical to this effect:

> DEAR SIR,
>   A story of mine, "The Yellow Wallpaper," was printed in your
> issue of May, 1891. Since you do not pay on receipt of ms. nor on
> publication, nor within six months of publication, may I ask if you
> pay at all, and if so at what rates?

They replied with some heat that they had paid the agent, Mr. Austin. He, being
taxed with it, denied having got the money. It was only forty dollars anyway! As a
matter of fact I never got a cent for it till later publishers brought it out in book form,
and very little then. But it made a tremendous impression. A protest was sent to the
Boston *Transcript*, headed "Perilous Stuff"—

To the Editor of the Transcript:

In a well-known magazine has recently appeared a story entitled "The Yellow Wallpaper." It is a sad story of a young wife passing the gradations from slight mental derangement to raving lunacy. It is graphically told, in a somewhat sensational style, which makes it difficult to lay aside, after the first glance, til it is finished, holding the reader in morbid fascination to the end. It certainly seems open to serious question if such literature should be permitted in print.

The story can hardly, it would seem, give pleasure to any reader, and to many whose lives have been touched through the dearest ties by this dread disease, it must bring the keenest pain. To others, whose lives have become a struggle against an heredity of mental derangement, such literature contains deadly peril. Should such stories be allowed to pass without severest censure?

M.D.

Another doctor, one Brummel Jones, of Kansas City, Missouri, wrote me in 1892 concerning this story, saying: "When I read 'The Yellow Wallpaper' I was very much pleased with it; when I read it again I was delighted with it, and now that I have read it again I am overwhelmed with the delicacy of your touch and the correctness of portrayal. From a doctor's standpoint, and I am a doctor, you have made a success. So far as I know, and I am fairly well up in literature, there has been no detailed account of incipient insanity." Then he tells of an opium addict who refused to be treated on the ground that physicians had no real knowledge of the disease, but who returned to Dr. Jones, bringing a paper of his on the opium habit, shook it in his face and said, "Doctor, you've been there!" To which my correspondent added, "Have you ever been—er—; but of course you haven't." I replied that I had been as far as one could go and get back.

One of the *New England Magazine's* editors wrote to me asking if the story was founded on fact, and I gave him all I decently could of my case as a foundation for the tale. Later he explained that he had a friend who was in similar trouble, even to hallucinations about her wallpaper, and whose family were treating her as in the tale, that he had not dared show them my story till he knew that it was true, in part at least, and that when he did they were so frightened by it, so impressed by the clear implication of what ought to have been done, that they changed her wallpaper and the treatment of the case—and she recovered! This was triumph indeed.

But the real purpose of the story was to reach Dr. S. Weir Mitchell, and convince him of the error of his ways. I sent him a copy as soon as it came out, but got no response. However, many years later, I met some one who knew close friends of Dr. Mitchell's who said he had told them that he had changed his treatment of nervous prostration since reading "The Yellow Wallpaper." If that is a fact, I have not lived in vain.

A few years ago Mr. Howells asked leave to include this story in a collection he was arranging—*Masterpieces of American Fiction*. I was more than willing, but assured him that it was no more "literature" than my other stuff, being definitely written "with a purpose." In my judgment it is a pretty poor thing to write, to talk, without a purpose.

All these literary efforts providing but little, it was well indeed that another avenue of work opened to me at this time.

CORRESPONDENCE

[Gilman's accounts of the story's publication and reception make reference to a great deal of correspondence: letters to and from William Dean Howells, Horace Scudder, Henry Austin, the editors of The New England Magazine, S. Weir Mitchell, and other doctors. Many of those letters no longer survive or remain to be discovered by other researchers. Reprinted here are letters that bear on the publication, republication, and reception of "The Yellow Wall-paper" from 1890 until 1934. I have also included letters that shed light on Gilman's dealings with Howells and with her publishers, Small, Maynard & Co. The letters are arranged chronologically, and the manuscript locations are given for each item. Unless otherwise noted, all letters are reprinted in their entirety.]

1. W. D. HOWELLS TO CPS, 9 JUNE 1890

Schlesinger Library, Gilman Papers, folder 120

[printed heading]   184 Commonwealth Avenue.
                                        Boston, June 9, 1890

Dear Madam:

I have been wishing ever since I first read it—and I've read it many times with unfailing joy—to thank you for your poem in the April Nationalist. We have had nothing since The Biglow Papers half so good for a good cause as Similar Cases.

And just now I've read in the Woman's Journal your Women of To-Day. It is as good almost as the other, and dreadfully true!

                                        Yours sincerely
                                        W. D. Howells.

[In her autobiography, Gilman calls Howells's letter "unforgettable," and recalls her reaction to his praise: "That was a joy indeed. I rushed over to show Grace and the others. There was no man in the country whose good opinion I would rather have had. I felt like a real 'author' at last" (Living, p. 113).]

2. CPS to W. D. Howells, 16 June 1890

Houghton Library, bMs Am 1784 (178)

> Box 401 Pasadena Cal.
> Mon. June 16th. 1890.

To Mr. Wm. D. Howells.
Dear Sir,

I thank you most sincerely for your kind note received this morning. Among all the pleasant things I had hoped for in my work this particular gratification was never imagined. And the best part of it is that there is not a man in America whose praise in literature I would rather win!

With genuine gratitude for a very genuine pleasure—

> Yours sincerely,
> Charlotte Perkins Stetson.

3. CPS to Martha Luther Lane, 27 July 1890 [excerpt]

Charlotte Perkins Gilman Letters,
Rhode Island Historical Society

When my awful story "The Yellow Wallpaper" comes out, you must try & read it. Walter says he has read it <u>four</u> times, and thinks it the most ghastly tale he ever read. Says it beats Poe and Doré! But that's only a husband's opinion.

I read the thing to three women here however, and I never saw such squirms! Daylight too. It's a simple tale, but highly unpleasant.

I don't know yet where it will be. If none of the big things will take it I mean to try the New York Ledger. Have you seen that in its new form? Kipling and Stevenson etc. etc. write for that now, so I guess I can.

4. W. D. Howells to Horace E. Scudder, 5 October 1890

Houghton Library, bMs Am 1784.1 (92)

Lynn, Oct. 5, 1890.

My dear Scudder:

The author wished me to send you this. It's pretty blood curdling, but strong, and is certainly worth reading—by you, I mean.

Mrs. Stetson is a relation of E. E. Hale's, I think, and she wrote that clever poem, Parallel Cases.

Yours ever
W. D. Howells

184 Com'th Ave.

5. Horace E. Scudder to CPS, 18 October 1890

Schlesinger Library, Gilman Papers, folder 126

[printed heading]
EDITORIAL OFFICE OF   18 October 1890
The Atlantic Monthly
BOSTON

Dear Madam

Mr. Howells has handed me this story. I could not forgive myself if I made others as miserable as I have made myself!

Sincerely yours
H. E. Scudder.

[At the top of the card, Gilman has penciled the note "(returning mss.)"]

6. W. D. Howells to CPS, 13 December 1891

Schlesinger Library, Gilman Papers, folder 120

[printed heading]
The Cosmopolitan Magazine
Editorial Department
New York, Dec. 13, 1891.

Dear Mrs. Stetson:

Do you think you could send me for this magazine something as good and wicked as Similar Cases, and of the like destructive tendency? And could you send it "on liking"?

Yours sincerely
W. D. Howells.

[In her diary for 21 January 1892 Gilman records sending two poems to Howells, "The Amoeboid Cell" and "The Cart before the Horse."]

7. W. D. Howells to CPS, 31 January 1892

Schlesinger Library, Gilman Papers, folder 120

[printed heading]
The Cosmopolitan Magazine
Editorial Department
New York, Jan. 31, 1892.

Dear Mrs. Stetson:

The Amoeboid Cell is so good that I think it deserves working over more carefully, and condensing a good deal. I don't like any part of the joke to be in the spelling, like "individualitee" and "anybodee," and I think your moral is a little too sharply pointed. Couldn't it be incidental, somehow? Perhaps I am over-particular, but then I always think I am worth pleasing, as an admirer of your gifts.

Yours sincerely,
W. D. Howells.

I am sorry I don't know about the [illeg.].

8. Dr. Brummell Jones to CPS, 12 April 1892

Schlesinger Library, Gilman Papers, folder 137

Kansas City Mo.
April 12th 1892.

My dear Miss Stetson.

There are so many good things in the public prints, that the appreciative soul is in continual hot water as to his duty in making personal acknowledgements. But the time that it would take, the question of propriety etc bring reflection, and reflection is a foe to action.

When I read "The Yellow Wall Paper" I was much pleased with it; when I read it again, I was delighted with it, and now that I have read it again I am overwhelmed with the delicacy of your touch and the correctness of portrayal. From a doctor[']s stand point, and I am a doctor, you have made a success. So far as I know, and I am fairly well up in literature, there has been no detailed, exact picture of incipient insanity. To begin with you have a delightful little woman to build upon, and you have handeled her tenderly. I was well into the story before I caught your drift, and I sometimes wonder if you knew how the poor thing was going. The continual recurence, under any and all circumstances, to the wall paper, with her grave chimerical talk; the gradual developement of the woman behind it, and the sudden transition of the woman into her own person is a master stroke; and the continuence of her creeping march over the body of her fainting husband is a grand climax.

Some time ago a gentleman called upon me in regard to the opium habit which he had contracted many years ago. As a number of physicians had treated him for it he was sceptical, and left me with the statement that physicians had no knowledge of the disease and that he would not be treated again. Next morning imagine my surprise to see him sitting in my office. He had in his hand a paper that I had written upon the opium habit, and as he arose to greet me he shook it in my face and said, "Doctor you've been there".

Have you ever been—er—; but of course you hav'nt.

Yours sincerely,
Brummell Jones.

1014 East Ninth St.

[Dr. Brummell Jones (1841–1923) practiced medicine in Kansas City from 1883 until 1912.]

9. CPS to George Houghton Gilman, 21 September 1897 [excerpt]

Schlesinger Library, Gilman Papers, folder 45; reprinted in *Journey*, p. 102.

Then Mr. [Sylvester] Baxter took me to his publishers—Small, Maynard & Co. And Co. was there. Who do you think Co. is? Bliss Carman! Wasn't I pleased to see him! They are all young fellows, Small a mere boy, and they regard my work with the eye of favor and want to publish 'em. At present they are publishing Whitman's works.

I, it appears, come next! I am to call again next Sat. morning, and they will make a definite proposition. Then I can see Mr. Ripley Hitchcock and talk quite big. It all seemed very nice and stimulating—I enjoyed it. Then I called on Mr. Edwin Meade at The New England office. He was delighted to see me—being a fellow Socialist, and having suffered much for my sake in publishing The Yellow Wallpaper—of which he spoke in extravagant terms. The Yellow Wallpaper and Similar Cases—these have made me apparently. He wants anything I'll send him, so if I can turn out some small stuff that I'm willing to part with for $2.50 a page—there's a market.

Bring on that bank—I'll open an account!

[Sylvester Baxter (1850–1927) was a minor poet, as well as a journalist and editor associated with several Boston newspapers. William Bliss Carman (1861–1929), sometimes called "Canada's poet laureate," published several of his nearly two dozen volumes of poems, songs, and essays with Small, Maynard & Co., and served as a director of the company after the retirement of Herbert Small in 1900. Acting on W. D. Howells's suggestion and endorsement, Gilman sent the manuscript of a volume of poetry to Ripley Hitchcock (1857–1918), the literary reader for D. Appleton & Co.; on 9 August 1897 Hitchcock offered to publish her book of poetry if she agreed to omit many of the poems from her San Francisco days (see W. D. Howells to CPS, 25 June 1897 and Ripley Hitchcock to CPS, 6 July 1897 and 9 August 1897, all in the Schlesinger Library, Gilman Papers, folder 120). Small, Maynard & Co. included those verses when they eventually published the enlarged third edition of In This Our World (1898).]

10. Clement R. Wood to CPG, 1 April 1912 [excerpt]

Schlesinger Library, Gilman Papers, folder 141

[Though he initially followed his father into a career as a lawyer in Birmingham, Alabama, Clement R. Wood (1888–1950) was a literary historian, best known for his anthologies and

histories of American poetry and his biography Amy Lowell: A Critical Life (1926). A year after graduating from Yale Law School, Wood wrote a long letter to Gilman to express his appreciation of her works and to ask her advice on how he could "be of most service" to humanity. The letter, which Gilman noted was "a prize worth working for," describes how reading her works led him to "acquire a soul" and embrace suffragism and socialism. Within two years, Wood relocated to New York and began his career as a teacher, poet, novelist, and leader of the American Association for the Advancement of Atheism. The following excerpts from the letter single out particularly influential works, including "The Yellow Wall-paper."]

And then the miracle happened. It merely consisted in my seeing a copy of "Our Man-made World" at the home of a friend, and picking it up and reading it. Up to that time, I had been entirely intolerant of the woman's movement; and that book, filled with examples drawn from facts within my knowledge, and brimful of wonderful truth and enlightenment, converted me at a bound from a commonplace grubber to one who has seen the vision.

Since then, I have read all of your works that I can lay my hands on, and have most of them in my library. "The Yellow Wall-Paper" is a flawless psychological masterpiece, and by far the best story of its kind that I have ever read. . . . "The Man-Made World", save for two curious lapses, as it seems to me, is a magnificent contribution to the literature of sociology, and in conclusion I may say that I have yet to read a line of yours that I do not agree with.

11. W. D. Howells to CPG, 7 October 1919

Schlesinger Library, Gilman Papers, folder 120

Kittery Point, Me.,
Oct. 7, 1919.

Dear Mrs. Gilman:

I hope you will like to let me use your terrible story of "The Yellow Wall Paper" in a book which I am making for Messrs. Boni & Liveright, and thinking of calling "Little American Masterpieces of Fiction." You will be in the best company I know, and I hope you will not curdle their blood past liquefying. I ~~hope~~ wish to give due recognition to the supreme awfulness of your story in my introduction.

Yours sincerely

W. D. Howells.

[Howells placed "The Yellow Wall-paper" at the head of the list of stories he wished to include in his collection, which was eventually titled Great Modern American Stories.]

12. CPG TO W. D. HOWELLS, 17 OCTOBER 1919

Houghton Library, bMs Am 1784 (178)

[printed heading of Forerunner magazine crossed out; THE FORERUNNER
CHARLOTTE PERKINS GILMAN'S MAGAZINE / CHARLTON CO., 67 WALL ST.,
NEW YORK]

627 W. 136.
Oct. 17. 1919

Dear Mr. Howells,

I am pleased and honored that you should wish to use <u>The Yellow Wallpaper</u> in the book as you ask. Did you know that that one piece of "literature" of mine was pure propaganda? I was once under Dr. Weir Mitchell's treatment, at 27. He sent me home to "Live as domestic a life as possible; have ~~my~~ your child with you all the time; lie down an hour after each meal; have but two hours intellectual life a day; (!) and <u>never touch pencil, brush, or pen as long as ~~I~~ you lived"</u>.

I tried it one summer, and went as near lunacy as one can, and come back.

So I wrote this,—and sent him a copy.

He made no response, but years after some one told me that he had told a friend "I have ~~completely~~ altered my treatement of neurasthenia since reading The Yellow Wallpaper." Triumph!

Please—did you ever receive either one of the bound volumes of the first year of my precious Fore-/<u>runner</u>? That first year was precious any how; fourteen numbers, and covers bound in. I did want you to notice my baby, and tried twice—letter and book.

As you may know I wrote that little magazine—all of it, for seven years. Stopped Dec. '16. Some of i[t] was pretty good. And it was a large piece of work any how;—21,000 wds a month. Also I had to work a lot more, on the side, to pay for the privilege of publishing a magazine! But I am well pleased. Some day I'll publish a lot of it, in book form. And I could not have accomplished so much work in the same time any other way!

Heres my last bit of verse, to amuse you.

Yours with grateful admiration and warm good will—
Charlotte Perkins Gilman.

13. EDITH FOSTER FLINT TO CPG, 23 NOVEMBER 1923

Schlesinger Library, Gilman Papers, folder 143

[Edith Foster Flint (1873–1949), professor of English at the University of Chicago, wrote this intriguing letter to Gilman after teaching "The Yellow Wall-paper" in her writing classes. At the top of the letter, Gilman has noted that Flint's letter was "ansd. promptly & at length," but that reply has not been located.]

[printed heading]

THE UNIVERSTIY OF CHICAGO

THE COLLEGES OF ARTS, LITERATURE AND SCIENCE

OFFICE OF THE DEAN

Mrs. Charlotte Perkins Gilman,
Care of The Century Co.,
New York.

My Dear Mrs. Gilman:—

I wonder if you would be so very good as to throw light on one element in The Yellow Wall Paper. It might be urged that, having written the story, you have done your share and more. But it is just because you have done so much, just because the tale is so amazingly effective, that one cares. The situation is this: for a year or more I have used The Yellow Wall Paper in a course in narrative writing as a powerful example of the story of emotional effect. It has been fun to watch students' reaction to it. But one point "remains greatly dark" to them and, I must confess, to me: what had been the previous use to which the yellow-papered room had been put? One really is in too much painful doubt. One remembers, creepily, Robert Frost's A Servant To Servants. And on the other hand, there's the long arm of coincidence.

A group of very eager readers, grateful to you for a very ugly jolt (that is a terrible ending), would deeply appreciate the kindness of an illumination by you.

Sincerely yours
(Mrs.) Edith Foster Flint

November 23, 1923

[In Robert Frost's dramatic monologue, "A Servant to Servants" (1914), a country wife tells her life's story to an outsider camped on her husband's land. The drudgery of her daily life, endlessly cooking and cleaning for her husband and the hired hands, has been relieved only by a brief stay in the State Asylum. She compares her institutionalization to the treatment of her insane uncle, who was kept locked in a cage within a room of an upstairs chamber.]

14. Mary L. Elting [*The Golden Book Magazine*] to CPG, 28 July 1931

Schlesinger Library, Gilman Papers, folder 126

[printed heading]
The / Golden / Book / Magazine / 55 FIFTH AVENUE / NEW YORK
EDITORIAL ROOMS

July 28, 1931.

Miss Charlotte P. Gilman,
380 Washington Street,
Norwichtown, Conn.

Dear Miss Gilman:—

We are sending you, under separate cover, a copy of the Golden
Book for January 1931, in which Mr. Fred Lewis Pattee mentions
"The Yellow Wallpaper" as one of the twenty best short stories.
We have never reprinted it in the Golden Book, but it is on our list
for one of our forthcoming issues. May we have your permission
to use it some time soon? We shall, of course, send you a small
acknowledgment check when the story appears.

Sincerely yours,
Mary L. Elting
The Golden Book.

[*The Golden Book Magazine* described its mission as "digging out from the past that which is
still vital and entertaining for modern readers and sifting from the present that which seems most
likely to endure" (vol. 13, January 1931, p. 4). Fred Lewis Pattee (1863–1950)—author
of *History of American Literature Since 1870* (1915), *Development of the American Short
Story* (1923), and *The Feminine Fifties* (1940), among other important volumes of criticism—
led the fight to establish American literature in the college curriculum. In 1918 he became the
country's first Professor of American Literature, a position he held at the Pennsylvania State
University until 1928 and later at Rollins College (1928–41) and Middlebury College's
Bread Loaf Summer Institute (1928–36). In addition to "The Yellow Wall-paper," Pattee's
list of America's twenty best short stories consisted of: "Rip Van Winkle," Washington Irving;
"The Murders in the Rue Morgue," Edgar Allan Poe; "The Ambitious Guest," Nathaniel
Hawthorne; "Life in the Iron Mills," Rebecca Harding Davis; "An Ingenue of the Sierras,"
Bret Harte; "The Turn of the Screw," Henry James; "The Courting of Sister Wisby," Sarah
Orne Jewett; "The Lady or the Tiger?" Frank R. Stockton; "Louisa," Mary E. Wilkins;
"At Teague Poteet's," Joel Chandler Harris; "The Cat of the Cane Brake," Frederick S.
Greene; "Chita," Lafcadio Hearn; "The Son of the Wolf," Jack London; "Desirée's Baby,"
Kate Chopin; "The Choice," Edith Wharton; "Vain Oblations," Katherine F. Gerould;

"A Municipal Report," O. Henry; "The Belled Buzzard," Irvin Cobb; and "The Yellow Cat," Wilbur Daniel Steele. Gilman gave the magazine permission to reprint "The Yellow Wall-paper" on 7 August 1931, and the story appeared in the October 1933 issue of The Golden Book, with a subheading calling it "One of the Greatest Horror Stories Ever Written by an American."]

15. CPG TO LYMAN BEECHER STOWE, 16 DECEMBER 1932 [EXCERPT]

Schlesinger Library, Beecher Stowe Collection, M-45, reel 6

[Gilman's cousin Lyman Beecher Stowe (1880–1963) was a successful lecturer and author of several books on the Beecher family. Gilman's correspondence with him often concerned ways to obtain speaking engagements or publication opportunities. The following excerpt reprints only the first page of her letter.]

Dec. 16th. '32

Dear Cousin Lyman,

"The Yellow Wallpaper" was included by Howells, in "<u>Masterpieces of American Fiction</u>", Boni, Livright & Co.; and in "<u>American Mystery Stories</u>", Oxford Press. I can bestow upon you one of the original copies — from The New England Magazine, also. And I never got a cent for it! An agent placed it & took the pay, <u>only $40.00</u>. I gave you a copy of ["]Perhaps,["] surely, but here is another one. Also here is a set of "River Windows".

16. CPG TO LYMAN BEECHER STOWE, 26 SEPTEMBER 1933 [EXCERPT]

Schlesinger Library, Beecher Stowe Collection, M-45, reel 6

[In the first part of this letter, Gilman tells Stowe of her recent speaking engagements in Chicago and her hopes for similar work in California and Oregon. Saying that she is "beginning to bestir myself and get out a little list of lectures and send 'em around," she speculates on whether "something could be done in New York." Six months later, when she has failed to arrange a lecture tour, she laments to her daughter that "I have no 'pull' anymore" (CPG to KBSC, 11 March 1934).]

It does seem as if in a city of that size, where there must be many who remember me[,] I might get a chance of some sort, if only a Parlor Talk.

Did you observe that The Golden Book for October has my

Yellow Wallpaper in it? If you haven't a copy of that pleasant tale here's your chance to get one for a quarter.

17. LYMAN BEECHER STOWE TO CPG, 19 OCTOBER 1933 [EXCERPT]

Schlesinger Library, Beecher Stowe Collection, M-45, reel 6

[Stowe's response to Gilman's letter of 26 September congratulates her on her recent appearances in Chicago, and responds to her queries about other lecturing opportunities. The following brief paragraph appears amid discussions of his own work and doubts about his ability to act as an intermediary with agents on her behalf.]

We eagerly bought a copy of the "Golden Book" for October in order to have "The Yellow Wall Paper". I am glad you are going to tackle the ethics again.

18. CPG TO LYMAN BEECHER STOWE, 2 NOVEMBER 1933

Schlesinger Library, Beecher Stowe Collection, M-45, reel 6

> 380 Washington St.
> Norwich Town Conn.
> Nov. 2nd. 1933.

Dear Lyman —

Thank you, I'll love to come to your home on Feb. 4th, always a pleasure to see you dear people. Look here, I've had an idea! I think I told you my "Yellow Wall Paper" came out in the Oct. <u>Golden Book</u>.

Why wouldn't that make a <u>gorgeous monologue</u>! Stage setting of the room <u>and the paper</u>, the four windows—the moonlight on the paper—changing lights, and <u>movement</u>—and the woman staring!

I could do it myself, in a drawing room and make everybody's flesh creep; but I think it would make a real Emperor Jones'y thing on the stage. I thought of Eva Le Gallien—could she do it? I've met her.

Perhaps Kate Hepburn would consider it—though she's pretty young. Oh if Nazimova would! She's not dead is she!?

Maybe your august Mama-in-law would know somebody—has she read it?

Well, I must scrabble along on the Ethics.

> Love to both of you —
> Cousin Charlotte

I wrote Alexander Black about it—he knows all kinds.

[The central scenes in Eugene O'Neill's The Emperor Jones *(1920) feature an expressionistic monodrama in which the title character relives his own and his race's history, progressively distorting objective reality to express a subjective inner reality. Actress Eva Le Gallienne (1899–1991)—founder, manager and director at New York's Civic Repertory Theatre (1926–32)—was known for presenting challenging and unusual plays, particularly those of Henrik Ibsen. Russian-born stage and silent film actress Alla Nazimova (1878–1945), a student of Stanislavski's at the Moscow Art Theatre, transformed the American theater at the end of the nineteenth century by bringing unusual emotional depth to the characters she played. Katharine Houghton Hepburn (b. 1907) was acquainted with Gilman through her mother, Katharine Martha Houghton, an active supporter of the women's and labor movements. During Hepburn's childhood, her mother frequently entertained such famous women as Emmeline Pankhurst, Emma Goldman, and Gilman in the family's West Hartford, Connecticut, home. Gilman was a great admirer of Hepburn's acting talents, and had seen her on stage several times (CPG to KBSC, 6 January 1934). Alexander Black (1859–1940), known as "the father of the photoplay," originated the idea of projecting pictures onto a screen and accompanying them with spoken narrative, thus paving the way for motion pictures.]*

19. LYMAN BEECHER STOWE TO CPG, 3 NOVEMBER 1933 [EXCERPT]

Schlesinger Library, Beecher Stowe Collection, M-45, reel 6

[This excerpt includes only the first paragraph of Stowe's letter; the remainder concerns his own difficulties with his book on the Beecher family.]

November 3, 1933

Dear Cousin Charlotte:

I should think the "Yellow Wallpaper" might make an excellent monologue although, of course, I know very little about such matters. Why not try Eva Le Gallienne or Nazimova, for that matter? I feel sure she is still living because only a year or two ago I read notices of a play which she was then doing. I will ask Mother Jennie if she has anyone to suggest, and if she has not read it, I will show it to her.

[Gilman's suggestion of a dramatization of "The Yellow Wall-paper" apparently went unfulfilled during her lifetime. The idea, however, did not die. On 27 November 1945, her daughter Katharine entered into a contract agreement with the Bender-Ward Agency in New York for the motion picture and radio rights to the story (Schlesinger Library, Grace Ellery Channing Stetson Collection, folder 225). In the past two decades there have been numerous stage and screen adaptations of "The Yellow Wall-paper." The story was staged nearly verbatim by director Warren Kliewer as a monologue performed by Michèle La Rue at the National Portrait Gallery and elsewhere during the 1980s.]

20. E[than] A[llen] Cross to CPG, 3 February 1934

Schlesinger Library, Gilman Papers, folder 146

[On letterhead of American Book Company, New York]

Dear Mrs. Gilman:

Years ago I read your short story entitled "The Yellow Wallpaper" and have seen it in story collections at least twice since. I think it is one of the finest studies of insanity in existence in fiction. I hope you will allow me to include this story in the revision and enlargement of my textbook on The Short Story.

Will you kindly address me in care of the American Book Company.

Sincerely yours,
E. A. Cross

[E. A. Cross (1875–1968) was a professor of Literature and English at the Colorado State College of Education (now the University of Northern Colorado). He edited several anthologies of literature for use in colleges and high schools, and was president of the National Council of Teachers of English (1940). Gilman granted him permission to reprint "The Yellow Wall-paper" in A Book of the Short Story (1934), and was sent a complimentary copy of the textbook on 27 November 1934.]

REVIEWS

[The following section includes essays occasioned by the publication or republication of "The Yellow Wall-paper." While most of the pieces are formal book reviews, those prompted by the story's initial publication are not; the first is an overview of the contents of the January 1892 issue of The New England Magazine, and the second is a letter to the editor of the Boston Evening Transcript. I include them here, rather than in the following section, because both represent responses to the story's appearance in print, not to Gilman's appearance as a lecturer.]

1. *The New England Magazine* (1892)

a. Anon., "January Magazines," *Boston Evening Transcript*, 1 January 1892, p. 6, col. 5 [excerpt].

[The column reviews the contents of The New England Magazine, which the editors call an "enterprising young magazine," and The Magazine of American History. I reproduce here only the final paragraph of the section on The New England Magazine.]

S. Q. Lapius contributes a fine poem, "The Gray Dawn." Edith Mary Norris has a powerful and pathetic story of the good old days of witchcraft, called "A Salem Witch." Charlotte Perkins Stetson contributes a story called "The Yellow Wallpaper," which is very paragraphic and very queer generally. One of Phillips Brooks's finest sermons on Abraham Lincoln is reproduced, with a commentary upon it by Mr. Mead. A number of other poems and sketches complete a very interesting number.

b. M. D., "Perilous Stuff," *Boston Evening Transcript*, 8 April 1892, p. 6, col. 2.

To the Editor of the Transcript: In a well-known magazine has recently appeared a story entitled "The Yellow Wallpaper." It is a sad story of a young wife passing through the gradations from slight mental derangement to raving lunacy. It is graphically told, in a somewhat sensational style, which makes it difficult to lay aside, after the first glance, til it is finished, holding the reader in morbid fascination to the end. It certainly seems open to serious question if such literature should be permitted in print.

The story can hardly, it would seem, give pleasure to any reader, and to many whose lives have been touched through the nearest ties by this dread disease, it must bring the keenest pain. To others, whose lives have become a struggle against an heredity of mental derangement, such literature contains deadly peril. Should such stories be allowed to pass without protest, without severest censure?

M. D.

2. *The Yellow Wall Paper*, Small, Maynard & Co., Boston, 1899

a. A[nne] M[ontgomerie], "The Yellow Wall Paper," *The Conservator* 10 (June 1899), pp. 60–61.

This story, which treats of the psychology of mental disorder, appeared some years ago (1892) in The New England Magazine and is now reprinted out of deference to the growing popular interest in the work of its author. Readers who wish further proof of the versatility of Mrs. Stetson need but to examine this monograph to be convinced. It is in style quite different from what may be considered her customary and contemporary, or in a sense even her most serious, mood, although the keen penetration and inevitable touch which characterize that is here also.

The Yellow Wall Paper seems at first to be only a skit—a gentle, mildly amusing joke. But it grows and increases with a perfect crescendo of horror. It is almost uncanny to come upon Mrs. Stetson in the act of making literature of this sort—she is so interested, heart and soul, in such other things as woman's economic status, and so identified with the philosophic assertion of sex independence. Here she is writing about a woman afflicted with nervous prostration. This woman tells her own story. She is taken for quiet and rest to a place in the country that can be described only by using all the adjectives of enjoyment in the language. But in this paradise she meets with one thing she does not like—a certain yellow wall paper. It is a condition, not a wall paper, of course. Anything would have served her fancy; if she had not referred her malady to that yellow wall paper it would have attached itself to some other phenomenon. It is a piteous recital. We reach a fatal but necessary crisis—the victim ceases to be a spectator of the baffling movements of the creeping woman behind the bars of the wall paper and herself becomes the creeper delighted to escape. The story is simple, serious, sly, fascinating, torturing. It is embodied excitement. It is brooding insanity. Imagine Mrs. Stetson tracing out curiously and deftly the lines of such a picture.

And the wall paper in prototype peers at you from the covers of the little book with staring bulbous eyes all over the livid orange and a sulphurous smooch at its base.

A. M.

[Anne Montgomerie (1864–1954) was the wife of the founder and editor of The Conservator, *Horace Traubel, whom Gilman had met the previous October.]*

b. Anon., "Book Reviews," *The Coming Nation* (Ruskin, Tennessee) 24 (June 1899), p. 4.

THE YELLOW WALL PAPER, by Charlotte Perkins Stetson, 55 pp. artistically printed and bound in boards, uncut edges, price 50 cents. Published by Small, Maynard &

Co., Boston. A strange, weird story, uncommonly fascinating. A beautiful gift book, that will be highly appreciated. A competent critic says: The Yellow Wall Paper, that strange study of physical environment, deservedly ranks as one of the most powerful of American short stories.

[A weekly socialist paper begun in 1893 by J. A. Wayland, The Coming Nation was subtitled "A Journal of Things Doing and To Be Done"; Wayland left in 1895 to found and edit Appeal to Reason, and A. S. Edwards continued as editor through 1899. On the same page as this review, the paper prints Gilman's poem "Charity," a brief review of the second edition of Women and Economics, and a notice entitled "Late Literary News" announcing Gilman's forthcoming article in The Cosmopolitan in which she rebuts Harry Thurston Peck's ideas about "The Woman of Today and Tomorrow." Gilman visited Ruskin, Tennessee, at the end of January, 1899, and wrote two articles for The Coming Nation in the spring of the same year.]

c. Anon., "New Books and Those Who Make Them," *Boston Daily Advertiser*, 10 June 1899, p. 8.

[The similarities between this and the following review suggest that reviewers may have received a press release from the publisher.]

A second edition of Mrs. Charlotte P. Stetson's "Women and Economics" has been brought out by Small, Maynard & Company. The text, except for a few slight corrections, remains the same, but a full index has been added.

The publishers have just issued Mrs. Stetson's story, published some years ago in one of the magazines. It is called "The Yellow Wall Paper." Those who were fortunate enough to read the tale when it first appeared will welcome it in book form, for there is no doubt that it is one of the most powerful and original short stories published for many years. It appears in a cover of orange and yellow, not beautiful in design, but purposely intended to represent the horrible wall covering that caused the insanity of the poor nervous invalid who was compelled to look at it day after day.

d. Anon., "Literary Gossip," *Boston Herald*, 10 June 1899, p. 8.

A second edition of Mrs. Charlotte Perkins Stetson's "Women and Economics" has been brought out by Messrs. Small, Maynard & Co. The text, except for a few unimportant corrections, remains the same, but a full index of subjects has been added. The same publishers are also issuing Mrs. Stetson's story, published some years ago in one of the magazines, "The Yellow Wall Paper." It will appear in a cover of orange and yellow, which it is hoped will be sufficiently suggestive of the uncommon quality of the story itself.

e. Anon., "A Question of 'Nerves.'" *[Times (?)]* (Baltimore, Md.), 10 June 1899.

A slight but suggestive study in neuroticism is "The Yellow Wall Paper," by Charlotte Perkins Stetson (Boston: Small, Maynard & Company). The writer, who has contributed a good deal of serious matter on the subject of social economics, has in this instance taken up the pen of the fictionist, "The Yellow Wall Paper" being the diary of a nervous woman driven insane by the stupid devotion of a husband and by living in a bedroom decorated with wall paper of "a smouldering, unclean yellow," having "one of those sprawling flamboyant patterns committing every artistic sin." To follow its outrageous writhings was "as good as gymnastics." The book is bound in what one may suppose is a sample of the abhorred paper, and its grotesque design will easily arouse sympathy for the poor lady. The story, far from being ridiculous, has a touch of ghastliness. After reading it the model husband will be inclined seriously to consider the subject of repapering his wife's bed chamber according to the ethics of William Morris.

f. Anon., *The American* (Philadelphia), 10 [?] June 1899.

A natural comment on a little story by Charlotte Perkins Stetson— a story that is strikingly original in idea and method—is that blood is bound to tell. She is a descendant of the Beechers, and the blood has lost nothing in character in the descent. She has already made a hit as a clear and thoughtful essayist, especially on subjects relating to modern social problems, including the part of woman in industrial life, subjects that have been discussed to rags, yet to which she brings a new interest. She has humor, of course, and she has art in a higher degree than the author of "Uncle Tom's Cabin." This is revealed in "THE YELLOW WALL PAPER," which first appeared in a New England periodical. It is now printed in a very thin book by Small, Maynard & Co.

In his long illness Alphonse Daudet suffered from nerves. He changed his room because he thought a figure on the frieze looked like the face of a vicious man. Others have remarked that certain quilt patterns or wall paper patterns were calculated to drive one crazy. It is known that they suggest strange fancies, which in the sick become positive delusions. This is the motive of Mrs. Stetson's story. A woman with nerves, the wife of a doctor and a young mother, relates the increasing influence over her mind of a complicated yellow wall paper pattern. At first she is both amused and distressed, but gradually she gives rein to her imagination, and at last develops a case of insanity. It is a wonderfully impressive and moving little sketch, and would alone prove the artist.

g. H[enry] B. B[lackwell], "Literary Notices: The Yellow Wall Paper," *The Woman's Journal*, 17 June 1899, p. 187.

This is a most striking and impressive study of morbid psychology, in the shape of a story. A woman goes insane through the effort of her husband, a well-meaning physician, to cure her of "a temporary nervous depression—a slight hysterical tendency" by keeping her confined in a quiet house, where she takes phosphates and tonics and air and exercise, but is absolutely forbidden to work. The poor woman believes that what she needs is congenial work, with excitement and change, less opposition, and more society and stimulus. She keeps a journal, and mopes. With frightful simplicity and naïvite she records from day to day her mind's gradual passage from melancholy to madness, which last takes its hue from a disagreeable yellow wall paper. With pathetic sadness she begins her story thus:

"It is seldom that mere ordinary people like John and myself secure ancestral halls for the summer. A colonial mansion, a hereditary estate, I would say a haunted house and reach the height of romantic felicity,—but that would be asking too much of fate. Still, I will proudly declare that there is something queer about it. John laughs at me, of course. John is practical in the extreme. He has no patience with faith, an intense horror of superstition, and he scoffs openly at any talk of things not to be felt and seen put down in figures. John is a physician, and *perhaps*—(I would not say it to a living soul, of course, but this is dead paper and a great relief to my mind)—*perhaps* that is one reason I do not get well faster. You see, he does not believe I am sick! And what can one do?"

Nothing more graphic and suggestive has ever been written to show why so many women go crazy, especially farmers' wives, who live lonely, monotonous lives. A husband of the kind described in this little sketch once said that he could not account for his wife's having gone insane—"for," said he, "to my certain knowledge she has hardly left her kitchen and bedroom in 30 years."

This story appeared some years ago in the *New England Magazine*, and attracted much attention. A distinguished alienist said to her: "It exactly describes the phenomena of mental disease. By what extraordinary power of imagination and sympathy have you been able to enter into the consciousness of these unfortunates?" Many years ago a story was published, entitled "Miserrimus." It described with frightful intensity the horrors of remorse which preyed upon the unhappy victim until he became the inmate of an insane asylum. Both these books deserve to be perpetuated and widely circulated.

H. B. B.

[Henry Brown Blackwell (1825–1909), an ardent supporter of the women's movement, edited the Woman's Journal from 1870 until his death. Blackwell, his wife Lucy Stone, and their daughter Alice Stone Blackwell were close friends of Gilman's from the time they met at the Woman Suffrage Convention in 1886. Blackwell also reviewed Women and Economics

(1898), The Home: Its Work and Influence (1903), Human Work (1904), and several of Gilman's lectures for the Woman's Journal; his daughter reviewed In This Our World (1893) and several of Gilman's essays for the same publication, and wrote for the Woman Citizen about What Diantha Did (1910). Frederick Mansel Reynolds's anonymously published novella Miserrimus (1832) is the first-person narrative of a man tormented by the memory of his relentless revenge against his beloved, who rejects him after he kills her brother in a duel. "I sometimes cannot refrain from fancying that I never could have perpetrated [my deeds]," says the narrator, "unless at the time I had been the pre-ordained victim of confirmed insanity" (p. 74).]

h. Anon., "Books: Light and Serious Stories," *Time and the Hour* 10 (17 June 1899), p. 9.

WITH wonderful word-selection drawing curves and blobs and goggling eyes, with none of the real facts of her story told, but all left to inference, with no plot at all, but the simple "un-narration" of the horrors of the beginnings of puerperal insanity, Charlotte Perkins Stetson has done work in "The Yellow Wall-Paper" (Small, Maynard & Co.), reprinted from the *New England Magazine*, in a startling cover, which should bind and hold her to more as good. It is not good to retail the facts which Mrs. Stetson has hinted at; they are the facts which come to some of us and shake reason, religion, and faith clean out of us. Conan Doyle had no right, say the outraged physicians, to write "Round the Red Lamp." Be it so: this story is calculated to prevent girls from marrying far more surely than Dr. Doyle's "Unto the Third Generation" attacked young men.

The beauty of the work lies in the handling entirely. The wall-paper of hideous color and pattern showed to the new mother, as she became insane, a sub-pattern which grew always clearer. It was the figure of a woman trying to escape through the meshes of the outer pattern, and it makes the reader feel that his own mind is slipping to read behind the mad woman's chatter—which is all the story—the horrible facts. It is a strong book, a little yellow book, a well-done, horrible book,—a book to keep away from the young wife.

[Time and the Hour (1896-1900) was a small, Boston literary magazine edited by Edwin M. Bacon; it published such authors as Margaret Deland, Robert Grant, Frank B. Sanborn, and Ruth McEnery Stuart. In Round the Red Lamp: Being Facts and Fancies of Medical Life (1894; reprint, New York: Appleton, 1929), Sir Arthur Conan Doyle (1859–1930) published fifteen stories "which attempt to treat some features of medical life with a certain amount of realism" (p. iii). Most of the tales portray doctors as heartless clinicians, too interested in science to pay attention to their patients' emotional needs. "The Third Generation" concerns a young baronet who discovers on the eve of his wedding that he has inherited a hideous and incurable disease from his debauched grandfather. Dr. Horace Selby offers his patient several ignoble ruses by which to break off his engagement, but the young man rejects both the

suggestions and the doctor's prescription; he dies that night in an "accident" a few blocks away from the doctor's consulting room.]

i. Anon., "Fresh Literature: Matters of Interest in the World of Letters," *Los Angeles Sunday Times* (illustrated magazine section), 18 June 1899, p. 14.

"The Yellow Wall Paper."

Charlotte Perkins Stetson's remarkable study in progressive mania, bearing the above title, which was first published some years ago in the New England Magazine, has been issued in book form. It is a grewsome, but wonderfully strong and vivid little story of how a woman, already ailing nervously, went crazy through constantly studying the pattern on the wall paper. Everybody who has ever been ill in a room, the walls of which were covered with a patterned paper, will appreciate the little book. It is done with great cleverness and with such constant keenness and sureness of artistic perception that the pleasure the reader takes in it for this reason counter-balances the grewsomeness of the story. It is told in the first person, and the gradual absorption of the woman in the problems of the wall paper, as her mania progresses, and the way in which she conceals the signs of her insanity, are done with great skill. But unless the publishers of the book wish to be responsible for a large crop of maniacs, they ought not to have covered it with what is apparently a reproduction of that fateful wall paper. After one glance at its pattern, one cannot wonder that the poor woman went crazy.

j. Anon., "Glances at New Books," *Chicago Daily News,* 21 June 1899, p. 10.

A long time ago a careless reader picked up a magazine and stumbled on "The Yellow Wall Paper," a short story by Charlotte Perkins Stetson. There was a story which actually made the shivers chase down one's spine; it was a scary tale and of the insidious kind which produces its effect slowly. The reader does not realize he is in the grasp of terror till many minutes after he has finished, so artfully is he shown the breaking down of the story-woman's mind. "The Yellow Wall Paper" is in the form of a haphazard diary written by a woman whose mind is giving way. She does not know her doom and neither do you at first till the suspicion becomes a sickening certainty with an end. There is a complicated wall paper in the bedroom and the woman worries over the pattern with fatal results. As a short story it stands among the most powerful produced in America, and now that it has been sent out in tiny book form it is destined to gain more notice. The cover design is very clever in conception. *[Promotional materials issued by Gilman's Charlton Co. after 1919 quote the first half of this review's penultimate sentence.]*

k. Charles Fletcher Lummis, "That Which Is Written," *Land of Sunshine*, July 1899, p. 120.

Charlotte Perkins Stetson's grim and powerful story, *The Yellow Wall-Paper*, is issued in a very handsome little volume by Small, Maynard & Co., Boston. 50 cents. *[Journalist and editor Charles Fletcher Lummis (1859–1928) founded Land of Sunshine in 1894 as a magazine dedicated to reporting on the life and history of the Far West. The magazine was considered Los Angeles's foremost monthly by the time it became Out West in 1902; it later merged with San Francisco's Overland Monthly. Gilman contributed several poems to the magazine, and Lummis included her name in the masthead's list of important stockholders and contributors. Her friend Grace Ellery Channing was the journal's Associate Editor.]*

l. Anon., "A Study of Physical Environment," *Times* (Boston), 9 July 1899 [?].

We owe sincerest thanks, all of us who like "a good thing," to Messrs. Small, Maynard & Co. for printing "The Yellow Wall Paper," for it is a strange study of physical environment as it also is an American shortcake of uncommon excellence. When I wrote shortcake just then—it is a curious psychological fact that over eating of lucious Cape Cod strawberries has undue influence on the mind—I meant short story, of course, and sincere apologies are offered Mrs. Charlotte Perkins Stetson, the author of this witty and sarcastic volume, for the error. There is not much to the book, size only considered, but the contents are important enough to make the 55 pages assume the largeness of a Webster "on a bridge." It is not a dull book, it was not written for any special purpose, and it is of absorbing interest, and it is undoubtedly a fact that the writer of it is a woman of enthusiasm and intelligence, as well as wit and wisdom.
[The article continues with biographical sketch of CPG, but does not return to "The Yellow Wall-paper."]

m. Anon., "Minor Fiction," *Literature* (American edition), n.s. 27 (14 July 1899), p. 18.

Seldom is a strong and original story compressed into so small a number of pages as is "The Yellow Wall-Paper" (Boston: Small, Maynard and Company). Mrs. Stetson's tale of the subtle creeping on of insanity may be read at a sitting, but the haunting effect of the gruesome, realistic diary kept by its helpless victim will cling to the memory for days. The heroine is the wife of a physician, who is singularly blind to the persistent and harrowing distress caused her by confinement in a large, airy room, which is papered with a loathsome fungus sort of yellow paper with innumerable spirals and arabesques and a general motive of toadstools in endless iteration, so that the deadly fascination of the walls finally completes the overthrow of the tottering reason. In many respects the story is worthy of a place beside some of the weird and uncanny masterpieces of Hawthorne and Poe.

[A portion of this review's final sentence appears in the publicity materials issued by Gilman's Charlton Co. after 1919.]

n. Anon., "Book Notes," *The Criterion* 21 (22 July 1899), p. 25.

"The Yellow Wall Paper" is a little story by Miss Charlotte Perkins Stetson, a lady of talent, who exhibits it in an unusual number of fields. This small volume (published by Small, Maynard & Company) contains an eerie tale of insanity that is uncommonly effective. Most attempts to work up insanity as "material" are ineffective; but here the progress from nervous sensitiveness to illusion, and on to delusion, is put before the reader so insidiously that he feels something of that same chill alarm for his own mental soundness that accompanies actual contact with lunatics. The thing is made to move quickly, too, and picturesque, which cannot usually be said of studies marked with a kindred psychological interest. It only lacks distinction of style (a thing Miss Stetson rarely achieves) to merit a more serious recognition than, as it is, it is likely to get.

o. Anon., "The Yellow Wall Paper," *The Literary World* (Boston) 22 (22 July 1899), p. 236.

It may not be exactly wholesome to read about how it feels to go crazy, but *The Yellow Wall Paper* is at least very interesting as well as pathetic. Charlotte Perkins Stetson is its author, and she has drawn an exceedingly vivid and compelling picture of mental sickness and hallucination. Perhaps the best or the worst of the sketch is the reasonable suggestion that the end might have been different if the sufferer had been treated more rationally.

p. Anon., "In Book Land," *Newport* (Rhode Island) *Daily News*, 27 June 1899, p. 3.

Charlotte Perkins Stetson has broken many a lance a-tilting against masculine pachydermatism, usually, nevertheless, with the honors of the tourney. It is not her wont to enter the lists merely to display her skill and the gleaming brilliance of her weapons; she fights for benefits, not praise.

At first thought "The Yellow Wall Paper" seems a purposeless and gruesome study of the beginnings of insanity, in the guise of a short story. It has all the power of Mrs. Stetson's brain behind its horrible fascination, and follows one ruthlessly, whether he will or no, with a shuddering comprehension of that unnecessary decay of the mental fibre. Yet those familiar with Mrs. Stetson's work know that she writes nothing meaningless, and guess that the author would rejoice if her lifting the surface from one woman's subdermal processes of thought should illuminate for some other blundering, well-intentioned male murderer the effect of a persistent aversion upon knotted and jangled nerves.

The story was originally published in the New England Magazine, and is now issued in covers which are a sulphurous attempt to incarnate the title. It will doubtless receive again the startled attention first accorded it in periodical literature.

3. *THE GREAT MODERN AMERICAN STORIES: AN ANTHOLOGY*, COMP. AND ED. WILLIAM DEAN HOWELLS (NEW YORK: BONI & LIVERIGHT, 1920)

[Most of the reviews of this collection focus their criticism on Howells's selection of stories. Though some reviewers lament the absence of O. Henry, Poe, and Hawthorne while others disagree with the choice of stories to represent individual authors, most laud the anthology for reissuing long-forgotten masterpieces and for exhibiting catholicity of taste. After noting Howells's "liberality" in including Dreiser's "The Lost Phoebe," one reviewer wonders "how long the Dreiserians would have pondered before admitting to their anthologies a short story by Mr. Howells" (The Weekly Review). All agree that the collection bears the marks of Howells's personal tastes, for good or ill. In addition to the pieces excerpted below, several brief reviews appeared which offered no mention of Gilman or her story: The Springfield (Massachusetts) Republican, 1 August 1920, p. 11a; Booklist 17 (October 1920), p. 33; "Briefer Mention," The Dial 69 (November 1920), p. 547; "New Books," The Catholic World 112 (November 1920), pp. 270–71.]

a. Brander Matthews, "Choosing America's Great Short Stories," *The New York Times Review of Books*, 18 April 1920, pp. 179, 182, 189 [excerpt].

[This long review by Brander Matthews (1852–1929) surveys theories of the short story offered by Poe, Bliss Perry, and others before turning to the collection in hand. After noting the absence of his own favorites and the obstacles to editorial choice imposed by copyright restrictions, Matthews praises the collection's "incessant variety" of short story types and claims that no previous anthology "has gathered into a single volume so many of the masterpieces of this fascinating form."]

. . . To list them all would take too long; but it is possible to catalogue a few: Hale's most ingenious fantasy "My Double and How He Needed Me"; Mark Twain's "Jumping Frog," Henry James's "Passionate Pilgrim," Bret Harte's "Outcast of Poker Flat," Hamlin Garland's memorable "Return of a Private," Mary Wilkins's "Revolt of Mother," Harris's "Tar Baby," Cable's "Jean-ah Poquelin," Madeline Yale Wynne's "Little Room" (as tantalizing as Stockton's "The Lady or the Tiger?") and Charlotte Perkins Stetson's "Yellow Wall Paper" (as grim and gruesome as her father's "Devil-Puzzlers" was diabolically philosophic).

["Devil-Puzzlers" (1877), a short story by Frederick Beecher Perkins (1828–99), tells of Dr. Hicok, a "positive, hard-headed, bold, and self-confident" physician who believes he can outwit Satan if given the chance to ask three questions. After the devil easily answers the doctor's two hardest philosophical queries, the doctor's pretty young wife stumps Satan with a question as to which side is the front of her new bonnet.]

b. Anon., "The Run of the Shelves," *The Weekly Review* 3 (18 August 1920), p. 154.

. . . These tales are all bound together by the observance of a seemliness which is also comeliness, but in other points their diversity is prodigious. One listens by turns to the cultivated voice of Mr. James, the confidential undertone of Miss Jewett, the bravuras of Mrs. Spofford, the "Help, Help" of Mrs. Gilman, the breathless whisper of Mr. Bierce, the charivari of Miss Tracy, the rat-tat-tat of E. E. Hale, the glug-glug-glug of Mark Twain, the silvery laugh of Mr. Aldrich, and the chuckle of Uncle Remus. Ought these things to be together? Sometimes they fairly suffer by proximity. . . .

c. Anon., "Books in Brief," *The Nation* 111 (28 August 1920), p. 251.

. . . The expected names are all represented here except that of Howells himself, whose modesty, though it was sure to do so, ought not to have excluded something of his own—The Magic of a Voice, perhaps, or The Angel of the Lord. Harriet Prescott Spofford, Henry B. Fuller, Edith Wyatt, Charlotte Perkins Stetson Gilman, Madelene Yale Wynn, Virginia Tracy, if not quite so confidently expected, abundantly make good their claims to be in this company, none of them more so than Mrs. Gilman, whose The Yellow Wall Paper is appallingly effective. . . .

d. Constance Mayfield Rourke, "The American Short Story," *The Freeman* 2 (6 October 1920), p. 91.

[Constance Rourke (1885–1941) surveys the anthology's representation of different types of the American short story, preferring the "untrammelled movement" of earlier stories to the "clipped, assured economy of latter-day methods." She classes "The Yellow Wall-paper" as a story which "approach[es] the contemporary type."]
. . . Mrs. Gilman's "Yellow Wall Paper" is one of the best available examples of the compact tale of terror with which American writers are so adept; but the final lines of the story make of it the *tour de force*, the adroit fiction rather than the true record. . . .

e. A[lexander] B[lack], "Books and Reading," [unidentified source], c. April 1920.

[A clipping of this review from an unidentified publication was supplied to Gilman by the author, Alexander Black. The clipping in the Gilman archive is badly damaged, but the review seems largely to repeat information from Howells's bibliographical introduction to the collection.]

. . . [Howells] tells us that Mrs. Perkins Gilman's horrifying tale, of a woman's slow progress into hopeless insanity, "The Yellow Wall Paper," was refused by Horace Scudder for the *Atlantic* as so terribly good that it ought never to be printed, but that he persuaded the *New England Magazine* to take it. . . .

4. AMERICAN MYSTERY STORIES, ED. CAROLYN WELLS (N.P.: OXFORD UNIVERSITY PRESS, 1927)

[In 1927 Oxford University Press's American Branch simultaneously issued two collections of stories edited by Carolyn Wells, American Detective Stories and American Mystery Stories. The volumes were usually reviewed together, hence the reviewers' tendency to compare the genres in these excerpts.]

a. Anon., "Brief Reviews," *The Daily Oklahoman* (Oklahoma City), 29 January 1928.

Fourteen stories that are on the way to becoming classics. Not always distinct from ghost and detective stories, mystery stories present riddles which work one into an agony of curiosity and sometimes horror as in the case of What Was It? [by Fitz-James O'Brien] and The Yellow Wall-Paper, by Charlotte Perkins Gilman, a study of madness as powerful as the best of Poe's tales.

b. Anon., "New Books in Brief Review," *The Independent* 120 (11 February 1928), p. 141.

. . . The mystery stories are distinctly superior. Besides the tales of Poe, we are given some very real horrors, including those two unequaled stories, "The Yellow Wallpaper" and "The Upper Berth" [by F. Marion Crawford].

c. Anon., "Mystery Anthologies," *New York Times Book Review*, 17 June 1928, p. 23.

All detective stories are, or should be, mystery stories, but all mysteries are not necessarily detective stories. Under the mystery classification are included stories of mysterious happenings, usually unexplained, and often touching on the supernatural. Many of them—all of those chosen by Miss Wells—are of the sort that are perhaps better classified as tales of horror.

[The reviewer singles out two stories by Poe as "outstanding" and then lists without comment the remaining stories in the collection.]

ADDITIONAL PUBLISHED COMMENTARY

[The comments collected here are all excerpts of larger articles, most of them sketches of Gilman's life and career. Several of the articles seem to have been occasioned by her lecture tours or other activities, and they may have been based on interviews with Gilman. Also included here is William Dean Howells's discussion of "The Yellow Wall-paper" from his "Reminiscent Introduction" to Great Modern American Stories. In all cases, I have excerpted only those portions of the articles that refer directly to "The Yellow Wall-paper."]

1. DI VERNON [ELIZA DOUGLAS KEITH], "CHARLOTTE PERKINS STETSON," *SAN FRANCISCO NEWS LETTER*, 28 MARCH 1891, P. 5.

[In March 1891, Gilman traveled to San Francisco, where she spent several months lecturing and reciting poems before the Women's Christian Temperance Union, The Century Club, the Ebell Society, and the Working Women's Club, among other organizations. This profile was written in response to Gilman's lecture on "The Coming Woman" at the convention of the Pacific Coast Woman's Press Association on 16 March 1891. The article is largely a biographical sketch of Gilman's education and accomplishments, and it is probably based on interviews with Gilman. The author appears not to have read "The Yellow Wall-paper," which remained unpublished until January of the following year. She may have heard the story read aloud, for Gilman's diary records that she read "The Yellow Wall-paper" to family and friends several times during the spring of 1891 (March 20, April 23). Di Vernon was the pen-name of Eliza Douglas Keith (1860– 1939), a San Francisco educator, suffragist, and journalist who later served as Grand President of the Native Daughters of the Golden West.]

As a writer of short stories Charlotte Perkins Stetson possesses a constructive skill, and a dramatic power peculiarly her own. Most of her stories are somewhat lurid, particularly those of a ghostly nature. "I return you your story," wrote Editor Scudder of the *Atlantic*, "because I should hate to make others as miserable as I have made myself by reading it." "The Yellow Wallpaper," for such is the title of the tale, is of a calibre to make the flesh of its readers creep with horror. But as the world has its proper proportion of people, who[,] like the youth in the German fairy tale, run through the fields of literature exclaiming, "Oh, if I could but Shiver," it is safe to assume that it will fit their fancy "like the paper on the wall."

[The German fairy tale is "The Youth Who Could Not Shudder," by the Brothers Grimm.]

2. ANON., "CHARLOTTE PERKINS STETSON," BOOK NOTES (NEW YORK), N.S. 2 (JANUARY 1899), PP. 10-12.

The years that followed, both before and after her return to the east, were filled with lectures and addresses, and marked by stories and by verses that strike a deeper note of human sympathy in some respects than even *The Biglow Papers* awoke, though they glow with the same spirit of wit and sarcasm. And *The Yellow Wall-Paper*, that strange study of psychoneurosis, deservedly ranks as one of the most powerful of American short stories.

[All but four sentences of this profile of Gilman are reprinted in the brochure issued by Small, Maynard & Co. to promote Women and Economics and In This Our World. The brochure predates the publisher's monograph edition of "The Yellow Wall-paper," mentioning the work only as a short story. The brochure slightly alters the text of this profile by describing "The Yellow Wall-paper" as a "strange study of physical environment," the wording used by two other reviewers (cf. pp. 105 and 110).]

3. ANON., "REMARKABLE LITERARY SUCCESS OF MRS. CHARLOTTE PERKINS STETSON," OAKLAND ENQUIRER, [C. NOVEMBER 1899]

[This profile follows the subheading "The Brilliant Lecturer and Author to Visit Oakland Next Month—Has Been Preparing a New Book." A handwritten note on the clipping in Gilman's archive reads "written by A. A. Ammon [?]", but the note does not appear to be in Gilman's hand.]

Besides "Women and Economics," Mrs. Stetson has published a volume of verses under the title "In This Our World," which has been widely read and commended by those who delight in wit and earnestness, of which William Dean Howells says: "It is the best civic satire which America has produced since the Biglow papers.["] Mrs. Stetson has also just brought out in book form her remarkable story, "The Yellow Wall Paper," which many people are ranking with the classic tales of Poe and Hawthorne. Her pen has also been kept busy at the command of publishers of the leading magazine publications of this country. . . .

[The quotation attributed to Howells actually comes from the brochure for Gilman's books, which paraphrases Howells's review of In This Our World. In his "Life and Letters" column for Harper's Weekly (15 January 1896, p. 79), Howells wrote that "since the Biglow Papers we have had no civic satire, that I can think of, nearly so good. . . . "; reviewing a later edition in an essay for The North American Review on "The New Poetry" (May 1899) he

*wrote that "since the Biglow Papers there has been no satire approaching it in the wit flashing
from profound conviction; but this comparison suggests a likeness which does not exist; the
humor and sarcasm of Mrs. Stetson, indeed, teach by parable, but not through character as the
Biglow Papers do" (p. 589).]*

4. CHARLES BAINBRIDGE, "CHOOSING WALLPAPERS," NATIONAL FOOD MAGAZINE 53 (MAY 1916), PP. 9–11.

Perhaps some of you remember a story called, "The Yellow Wallpaper," by
Charlote Perkins Gilman. It is a good story and should be read by every house-
holder. I will go farther and aver that every housebuilder who papers a house for sale
or rent, ought to be *made* to read that story. If he refuses, he should be tied hand and
foot and obliged to listen while it is first read and then *sung* to him, for the man who
wouldn't listen gladly would be just the man who would inflict a "Yellow wallpaper" on a defenceless prospective tenant.

The Yellow wallpaper was a hideous, grimy, jeering face that forever leered upon
you from the design on the wall and it made a woman mad.

We have all seen papers that we felt sure would drive us mad if we had to look at
them long enough and steadily enough. It is very easy to imagine features into almost
any wallpaper design except those of the most definite of geometrical patterns, or of
the faint indistinguishable tracery type. This is especially true when one is ill or
convalescent, and a grinning gargoyle leering at you from a thousand different points
when even the inoffensive grasshopper is a burden, will drum a tune on tired nerves
that devils dance to. . . .

In the treatment of the bedroom walls one may be allowed greater latitude in the
selection of pretty papers, although here is where we must look out for the "yellow
wallpaper." Strong designs are to be avoided. They grow monotonous, and faces are
apt to leer from the best regulated of blossoms.

*[The bulk of the article discusses principles of wallpaper selection. National Food Magazine
began as What to Eat (1900–1908) and was absorbed by Table Talk in 1916.]*

5. WILLIAM DEAN HOWELLS, FROM "A REMINISCENT INTRODUCTION," THE GREAT MODERN AMERICAN STORIES: AN ANTHOLOGY (NEW YORK: BONI & LIVERIGHT, 1920), P. VII.

It wanted at least two generations to freeze our young blood with Mrs. Perkins
Gilman's story of *The Yellow Wall Paper*, of which Horace Scudder (then of *The
Atlantic*) said in refusing it that it was so terribly good that it ought never to be
printed. But terrible and too wholly dire as it was, I could not rest until I had

corrupted the editor of *The New England Magazine* into publishing it. Now that I have got it into my collection here, I shiver over it as much as I did when I first read it in manuscript, though I agree with the editor of *The Atlantic* of the time that it was too terribly good to be printed.

6. Alexander Black, "The Woman Who Saw It First," *The Century Magazine* 107 (November 1923), pp. 33-42.

[This long tribute to Gilman was penned by her close friend Alexander Black. See also Black's review of Howells's 1920 anthology (page 114) and Gilman's letter of 2 November 1933 to Lyman Beecher Stowe (page 100).]

It was after consulting Dr. Weir Mitchell, and being told by him that her nerves demanded absolute abstinence from all intellectual work, that she wrote "The Yellow Wall Paper," which Howells gathered into his "The Great Modern American Stories." Weir Mitchell was to be her audience, and it is certain that his reading of the story influenced all of his later methods of treating neurasthenia. When the story, as a work of art, came in for many honors, she remarked: "I wrote it to preach. If it is literature, that just happened."

Here you have a hint of her philosophy as a literary workman. There is a good deal the effect of maintaining that, having one's idea, the transmission of it may be left to the grace of God. That the thing might be the other way about — that the idea might be by the grace of God and the expression remain a matter of momentous individual responsibility — would not strike her as tenable if it implied close consciousness in writing. She can fling an idea into an art package without the slightest anxiety as to its possible loss in the mail. To argue that the primary importance of the idea is not contradicted by the integrity of the house in which it is to live, and that certain ideas may really deserve a temple, is never impressive to a believer in the righteousness of free-striding thought. Perhaps success in talking to audiences eye to eye breeds impatience with the technic of the written page, and written pages that have nothing but technic supply arguments enough to literary rebels. They are not good arguments. A literary house out of plumb, a temple with a leaky roof, do not praise impulse. To put it another way, a gorgeous art chariot without a passenger can be ludicrous, but, on the other hand, a noble ambassador deserves something better than a rickety vehicle in which to reach his appointed destination.

Such criticism would be less valid if Mrs. Gilman's resources were not so plainly to be seen. In her early writings, in parody and in analysis, she displayed real artistic virtuosity. She has a deep sense of beauty. This may often be repressed, or held in subjection to the scientific spirit, but its reality is never to be doubted. Her knowledge of verse forms and her use of them, whimsically or emotionally, indicate an uncommon equipment. In all of her writing the frequency with which she is able to bring a stinging clearness to crises of her thought convicts her at other times of a rushing indifference to form and to effectiveness. Thus in the enormous volume of writing she poured into her magazine, "The Forerunner," which for a fertile seven years she wrote from cover to cover, and which included two thought-crammed novels of great significance, "What Diantha Did" and "The Crux," she often sacrificed much to a pace of expression.

When Mrs. Gilman says, "I am not an artist," she is rebuking strictly esthetic expectations. A thing like "The Yellow Wall Paper" (there is many another) proves that she *is* an artist when she chooses. She has interests sterner than esthetics. . . .

Appendix: Printings of "The Yellow Wall-paper," 1892–1997

The following chronological list offers a partial record of the printings and reprintings of "The Yellow Wall-paper" since 1892. For the years before 1973 I have listed all texts that a thorough bibliographic search could discover. I include those texts recorded by Gary Scharnhorst (*Charlotte Perkins Gilman: A Bibliography*, Scarecrow Author Bibliographies, no. 71 [Metuchen, N.J.: Scarecrow Press, 1985], p. 60), as well as those listed in *Short Story Index* and other general fiction bibliographies. For the years since 1973, this list should be regarded as representative, not exhaustive, since the exact number of reprintings in anthologies can never be known. I have tried to include all known trade editions that made the story available to the general reader, along with a sampling of the most current editions of college textbooks on American literature, fiction, women's studies, and composition. Not all the texts have been fully collated, but I have traced each reprinting to a "source" text, the branch of the textual family tree from which it ultimately derives. Departures from the source text are noted, as are important variant readings. I have also corrected errant dates, names, and source identifications.

1892

"The Yellow Wall-Paper." *The New England Magazine*, n.s. 5 (January), 647–56.

1899

The Yellow Wall Paper. Boston: Small, Maynard & Company.

1901

Reissue of SM (1899)

1911

Reissue of SM (1899)

1920

Howells, W. D., ed. *The Great Modern American Stories: An Anthology*. New York: Boni and Liveright, pp. 320–37.
[Source: NE]

1922

"The Yellow Wall-paper." *New York Evening Post*, 21 January, pp. 9, 12.
[Source: NE. Sixteen sections.]

1927

Wells, Carolyn, ed. *American Mystery Stories*. N.p.: Oxford University Press, American Branch, pp. 176–97.
[Source: NE. 29.9, "expects that in men."]

1933

"The Yellow Wall-Paper." *The Golden Book Magazine* 18 (October), 363–73.
[Source: CW. Ten sections.]

1934

Cross, E[than] A[llen], ed. *A Book of the Short Story*. New York: American Book Company, pp. 400–413.
[Source: GB. Nine sections. 42.20, "in spite of you and Jennie!"]

1937

Laing, Alexander, ed. *The Haunted Omnibus*. Illustrations by Lynd Ward. New York: Farrar & Rinehart, pp. 55–72.
[Source: SM. Eleven sections. 42.20, "in spite of you and Jennie!" Misdates NE as 1895.]

1938

Ferguson, [John] De Lancey, Harold A[rlo] Blaine, and Wilson R[andle] Dumble, eds. *Theme and Variation in the Short Story*. New York: Cordon, pp. 111–29.
[Source: Cross (1934). Nine sections. 42.20, "in spite of you and Jennie!"]

1941

Laing, Alexander, ed. *Great Ghost Stories of the World: The Haunted Omnibus*. Garden City, N.Y.: Blue Ribbon Books. Reprint of *The Haunted Omnibus* (1937).
[Source: SM. Eleven sections. 42.20, "in spite of you and Jennie!"]

1942

Stern, Philip Van Doren, ed. *The Midnight Reader: Great Stories of Haunting and Horror*. New York: Holt, pp. 342–62.
[Source: SM. Ten sections. 42.20, "in spite of you and Jennie!"]

1943

Reed, Helene, ed. *About Women: A Collection of Short Stories*. Cleveland and New York: World Publishing, pp. 84–100.
[Source: SM. Ten sections.]

1948

Stern, Philip Van Doren, ed. *The Midnight Reader*. London: World Distributors, pp. 211–29. [Abridged paperback edition of *The Midnight Reader* (1942); "Originally published as a bound edition by The Bodley Head, London."]
[Source: SM. Nine sections. 38.8, "find it out by myself!"; 42.20, "in spite of you and Jennie!"]

1950

Davenport, Basil, ed. *Ghostly Tales to Be Told*. New York: Dodd, Mead & Company, pp. 238–58.
[Source: SM. Misdates the story's first appearance as 1895. 42.20, "in spite of you and Jennie!"]

1961

Wollheim, Donald A., ed. *More Macabre*. New York: Ace Books, pp. 65–82. Paperback.
[Source: SM. Ten sections. 42.20, "in spite of you and Jennie!"]

1965

Hadfield, John, ed. *A Chamber of Horrors: An Anthology of the Macabre in Words and Pictures*. Boston: Little, Brown, pp. 163–76.
[Source: NE. Ten sections. 42.20, "in spite of you and Jennie!"]

1966

Rabkin, Leslie Y., ed. *Psychopathology and Literature*. San Francisco: Chandler Publishing Company, pp. 95–111.
[Source: NE. A footnote at 42.20 in the present text reads: " 'Jane?' in the original text. The '?' may have been a printer's effort to warn proofreaders of a possible error. 'Jane' may be the narrator. Or 'Jennie' may be intended" (p. 111).]

1967

Wright, Lee, and Richard G. Sheehan, eds. *These Will Chill You: Twelve Terrifying Tales of Malignant Evil*. New York: Bantam, pp. 6–21. Paperback.
[Source: SM. Ten sections. 42.20, "in spite of you and Jennie!"]

1971

Manley, Seon, and Gogo Lewis, eds. *Ladies of Horror: Two Centuries of Supernatural Stories by the Gentle Sex*. New York: Lothrop, Lee & Shepard Company, pp. 138–55.
[Source: SM. Misdates the story as 1896. 42.20, "in spite of you and Jennie!"]

1972

Ghidalia, Vic, ed. *Eight Strange Tales*. Greenwich, Conn.: Fawcett, pp. 107–22. Paperback.
[Source: SM. Eleven sections. 42.20, "in spite of you and Jennie!" Introduction misdates NE as 1895.]

Hemley, Elaine Gottlieb, ed. *The Writer's Signature: Idea in Story and Essay*. Glenview, Ill.: Scott, Foresman and Company, pp. 87–99.
[Source: WDH]

Parker, Gail, ed. *The Oven Birds: American Women on Womanhood, 1820–1920*. New York: Anchor Books, pp. 317–34.
[Source: CW. Misdates the story's first appearance as 1891. 29.9, "but one expects that in [him]."]

1973

Hedges, Elaine, ed. *The Yellow Wallpaper*. New York: The Feminist Press at The City University of New York.
[*Source: NE. Copyright page misidentifies the text as SM.*]

1975

Kahn, Joan, ed. *Open at Your Own Risk*. Boston: Houghton Mifflin, pp. 1–17.
[*Source: CW. 29.9–10, "but one expects that in John, who is practical in the extreme.";*
42.20, "in spite of you and Jennie." Identifies the author as "Charlotte Curtis Stetson
Gilman."]

1976

Liebman, Arthur, ed. *Ms. Mysteries: Nineteen Tales of Suspense Written by Women and Featuring Female Heroines*. New York: Washington Square Press, pp. 100–121.
[*Source: SM. Ten sections. 42.20, "in spite of you and Jennie!"*]

1977

Dean, Nancy, and Myra Stark, eds. *In the Looking Glass: Twenty-One Modern Short Stories by Women*. New York: Putnam's, pp. 43–60.
[*Source: Parker (1972). 29.9, "one expects that in [him]." Cites FP as source on copyright page. The Introduction misdates NE as 1891; the Biographical Note gives the correct date, but lists 1900 as Gilman's death date.*]

1979

Wolf, Leonard, ed. *Wolf's Complete Book of Terror*. New York: Clarkson N. Potter; distributed by Crown, pp. 270–82.
[*Source: FP. Nine sections.*]

1980

Lane, Ann J., ed. *The Charlotte Perkins Gilman Reader: "The Yellow Wallpaper" and Other Fiction*. New York: Pantheon Books, pp. 3–19.
[*Source: GB via Ferguson (1938). Seven sections.*]

1983

Richter, David H., ed. *The Borzoi Book of Short Fiction*. New York: Knopf, pp. 382–94.
[*Source: GR. Six sections.*]

1984

Muller, Marcia, and Bill Pronzini, eds. *Witches' Brew: Horror and Supernatural Stories by Women*. Macmillan Midnight Library. New York: Macmillan, pp. 37–55.
[*Source: SM. Ten sections. Misdates NE as 1895. 42.20, "in spite of you and Jennie!"*]

1985

Bendixen, Alfred, ed. *Haunted Women: The Best Supernatural Tales by American Women Writers*. New York: Frederick Ungar, pp. 92–104.
[*Source: GR. Source misidentified as NE.*]
Gilbert, Sandra M. and Susan Gubar, eds. *The Norton Anthology of Literature by Women: The Tradition in English*. New York: Norton, pp. 1148–61.
[*Source: GR. Nine sections. Misdates NE as May 1892.*]

1987

Hartwell, David G., ed. *The Dark Descent*. New York: Tor, pp. 460–71.
[*Source: FP. Ten sections.*]

1988

Prescott, Peter S., ed. *The Norton Book of American Short Stories*. New York: Norton, pp. 137–50.
[*Source: NE*]
Ryan, Alan, ed. *Haunting Women*. New York: Avon Books, pp. 56–74.
[*Source: SM. Seven sections. 42.20, "in spite of you and Jennie!"*]

1989

Phillips, Robert, ed. *Triumph of the Night: Tales of Terror and the Supernatural by 20th Century Masters*. New York: Carroll & Graf, pp. 31–46.
[*Source: GR. Twelve sections (and some substantives) follow NE.*]
Schwartz, Lynne Sharon, ed. *The Yellow Wallpaper and Other Writings by Charlotte Perkins Gilman*. New York: Bantam, pp. 1–20.
[*Source: FP. Ten sections.*]

1990

Manguel, Alberto, ed. *Black Water 2: More Tales of the Fantastic.* New York: Clarkson Potter, pp. 762–79.
[*Source: SM. Omits line 29.26 and inserts a section break instead.*]

Wolff, Cynthia Griffin, ed. *Four Stories by American Women.* New York: Penguin, pp. 39–57.
[*Source: GR*]

1991

Elliott, Emory, et al., eds. *American Literature: A Prentice-Hall Anthology.* Englewood Cliffs, N.J.: Prentice Hall, 2: 654–65.
[*Source: NE*]

Miller, James E., Jr., ed. *Heritage of American Literature.* New York: Harcourt Brace Jovanovich, 2: 507–16.
[*Source: NE*]

Ostrom, Hans, ed. *Lives and Moments: An Introduction to Short Fiction.* Fort Worth, Tex.: Holt, Rinehart and Winston, pp. 193–204.
[*Source: GR. The text is reproduced without section breaks.*]

Phillips, Robert, ed. *The Omnibus of 20ᵗʰ Century Ghost Stories.* New York: Carroll & Graf, pp. 31–46. Softcover reprint of *Triumph of the Night* (1991).
[*Source: GR. Twelve sections.*]

Salmonson, Jessica Amanda, Isabelle D. Waugh, and Charles Waugh, eds. *Wife or Spinster: Stories by Nineteenth-Century Women.* Camden, Maine: Yankee Books, pp. 69–83.
[*Source: FP*]

1992

Adams, Bronte, and Trudi Tate, eds. *That Kind of Woman.* New York: Carroll and Graf, pp. 143–62.
[*Source: FP. Ten sections.*]

Baldick, Chris, ed. *The Oxford Book of Gothic Tales.* Oxford: Oxford University Press, pp. 249–53.
[*Source: FP. Ten sections.*]

Bergman, David, and Daniel Mark Epstein, eds. *The Heath Guide to Literature*, 3ᵈ ed. Lexington, Mass.: D. C. Heath, pp. 148–60.
[*Source: FP. Ten sections.*]

Birkerts, Sven, ed. *The Longwood Introduction to Fiction.* Boston: Allyn and Bacon, pp. 387–400.
[*Source: GR*]

Golden, Catherine, ed. *The Captive Imagination: A Casebook on* The Yellow Wallpaper. New York: The Feminist Press at The City University of New York, pp. 24–41.
[Source: FP. A source note misidentifies the text as SM (p. 24). Ten sections. The lines missing from FP (39.33–34) are restored in a footnote that mistakenly claims the lines appeared in NE and did not appear in SM.]

Oates, Joyce Carol, ed. *The Oxford Book of American Short Stories.* Oxford and New York: Oxford University Press, pp. 154–69.
[Source: CW. 29.9, "but one expects that in man."]

Solomon, Barbara H., ed. *Herland and Selected Stories by Charlotte Perkins Gilman.* New York: Signet, pp. 164–80.
[Source: GR]

1993

Erskine, Thomas L., and Connie L. Richards, eds. *The Yellow Wallpaper.* Women Writers: Texts and Contexts Series. New Brunswick, N.J.: Rutgers University Press, pp. 29–50.
[Source: FP and GR. Footnote misidentifies the text as NE. Six sections.]

Guth, Hans P., and Gabriele L. Rico, eds. *Discovering Fiction.* Englewood Cliffs, N.J.: Prentice Hall, pp. 196–206.
[Source: NE. Beginning with the second section, the editors number the sections from I to XI.]

Kirszner, Laurie G., and Stephen R. Mandell, eds. *Fiction: Reading > Reacting > Writing.* Fort Worth, Tex.: Harcourt Brace, pp. 155–68.
[Source: NE. The text is misdated 1899.]

May, Charles E., ed. *Fiction's Many Worlds.* Lexington, Mass.: D. C. Heath, pp. 362–74.
[Source: NE]

McMichael, George, et al., eds. *The Concise Anthology of American Literature,* 3ᵈ ed. Englewood Cliffs, N.J.: Prentice Hall, pp. 1539–50.
[Source: GR]

McQuade, Donald, et al., eds. *The Harper American Literature,* 2ᵈ ed. N.Y.: Harper-Collins, 2: 713–24. [Compact 2ᵈ ed., pp. 1771–82.]
[Source: GR. Compact 2ᵈ edition presents the story in six sections.]

Pickering, James H., ed. *Fiction 50: An Introduction to the Short Story.* New York: Macmillan, pp. 314–25.
[Source: NE. Beginning with the second section, the editor numbers the sections from I to XI.]

Rubenstein, Roberta, and Charles R. Larson, eds. *Worlds of Fiction.* New York: Macmillan, pp. 387–98.
[Source: GR]

Showalter, Elaine, ed. *Daughters of Decadence: Women Writers of the Fin-de-Siècle.* New Brunswick, N.J.: Rutgers University Press, pp. 98–117.
[Source: FP. Ten sections. Misdates NE as May 1892.]

Vesterman, William, ed. *Literature: An Introduction to Critical Reading.* New York: Harcourt Brace, pp. 87–100.
[Source: NE]

Young, Diana, ed. *The Situation of the Story: Short Fiction in Contemporary Perspective.* Boston: Bedford Books, pp. 301–15.
[Source: GR. Six sections.]

1994

Annas, Pamela J., and Robert C. Rosen, eds. *Literature and Society: An Introduction to Fiction, Poetry, Drama, Nonfiction,* 2^d ed. Englewood Cliffs, N.J.: Prentice Hall, pp. 337–49.
[Source: GR. Six sections.]

Baym, Nina, et al., eds. *The Norton Anthology of American Literature,* 4th ed. New York: Norton, 2: 645–57.
[Source: GR. Twelve sections follow NE. A source note misidentifies the text as NE (p. 645).]

Bohner, Charles H., ed. *Short Fiction: Classic and Contemporary.* 3^d ed. Englewood Cliffs, N.J.: Prentice Hall, pp. 359–69.
[Source: GR. Five sections.]

Hurt, James, ed. *Literature: A Contemporary Introduction.* New York: Macmillan, pp. 503–13.
[Source: NE]

Knight, Denise D., ed. *"The Yellow Wall-Paper" and Selected Stories of Charlotte Perkins Gilman.* Newark: University of Delaware Press, pp. 39–53.
[Source: AMS]

Lauter, Paul, et al., eds. *The Heath Anthology of American Literature,* 2^d ed. Lexington, Mass.: D. C. Heath, 2: 801–12.
[Source: NE]

Litz, A. Walton, ed. *Major American Short Stories,* 3^d ed. New York: Oxford University Press, pp. 286–300.
[Source: NE. Eleven sections.]

Perkins, Barbara, Robyn Warhol, and George Perkins, eds. *Women's Work: An Anthology of American Literature.* New York: McGraw-Hill, pp. 640–50.
[Source: GR]

Solomon, Barbara H., ed. *Rediscoveries: American Short Stories by Women: 1800–1916.* New York: Mentor, pp. 480–96.
[Source: FP. Ten sections.]

Trimmer, Joseph F., and C. Wade Jennings, eds. *Fictions*, 3ᵈ ed. New York: Harcourt Brace, pp. 460–70.

[*Source: GR. 42.20, "in spite of you and Jennie."*]

1995

Bain, Carl E., Jerome Beaty, and J. Paul Hunter, eds. *The Norton Introduction to Literature*, 6ᵗʰ ed. New York: Norton, pp. 569–81.

[*Source: NE*]

Bogarad, Carley Rees, and Jan Zlotnik Schmidt, eds. *Legacies: Fiction, Poetry, Drama, Nonfiction*. Fort Worth, Tex.: Harcourt Brace, pp. 662–75.

[*Source: GR*]

Cassill, R. V., ed. *The Norton Anthology of Short Fiction*, 5ᵗʰ ed. New York: Norton, pp. 679–93. [Shorter 5ᵗʰ ed., pp. 403–17.]

[*Source: GR. Twelve sections follow NE. A source note misidentifies the text as NE (p. 679).*]

Charters, Ann, ed. *The Story and Its Writer: An Introduction to Short Fiction*, 4ᵗʰ ed. Boston: Bedford Books, 1995, pp. 531–42. [Compact 4ᵗʰ ed., pp. 303–14.]

[*Source: GR. Seven sections, but 31.15 and 35.35 fall at page breaks.*]

Kennedy, X. J., and Dana Gioia, eds. *An Introduction to Fiction*, 6ᵗʰ ed. New York: HarperCollins, pp. 424–36.

[*Source: GR. Five sections.*]

Kennedy, X. J., and Dana Gioia, eds. *Literature: An Introduction to Fiction, Poetry, and Drama*, 6ᵗʰ ed. New York: HarperCollins, pp. 424–36. [Compact 6ᵗʰ ed., pp. 377–89.]

[*Source: GR. Five sections.*]

Moffett, James, and Kenneth R. McElheny, eds. *Points of View: An Anthology of Short Stories*. New York: Mentor, pp. 138–54.

[*Source: FP. Ten sections. 42.20, "in spite of you and Jennie."*]

Pickering, James H., ed. *Fiction 100: An Anthology of Short Stories*, 7ᵗʰ ed. Englewood Cliffs, N.J.: Prentice Hall, pp. 481–92.

[*Source: NE. Beginning with the second section, the editor numbers the sections from I to XI.*]

Rabkin, Eric S., ed. *Stories: An Anthology and an Introduction*. New York: Harper-Collins, pp. 443–54.

[*Source: NE*]

Roberts, Edgar V., and Henry E. Jacobs, eds. *Fiction: An Introduction to Reading and Writing*, 4ᵗʰ ed. Upper Saddle River, N.J.: Prentice Hall, pp. 491–502.

[*Source: GR. Five sections.*]

Shulman, Robert, ed. *The Yellow Wall-Paper and Other Stories*. Oxford and New York: Oxford University Press, pp. 3–19.

[*Source: NE. The Introduction and Note on the Text both correctly date the story's first appearance, but the source note accompanying the story itself misdates it as January 1890.*]

Wagner-Martin, Linda, and Cathy N. Davidson, eds. *The Oxford Book of Women's Writing in the United States*. Oxford and New York: Oxford University Press, pp. 41–55.
[*Source: NE. Eleven sections. The headnote misdates story as 1893, but the date at the end of story is correct.*]

1996

Anstendig, Linda, and David Hicks, eds. *Writing Through Literature*. Upper Saddle River, N.J.: Prentice Hall, pp. 842–55.
[*Source: NE*]

Beaty, Jerome, ed. *The Norton Introduction to Fiction*, 6th ed. New York: Norton, pp. 641–53.
[*Source: NE*]

Clayton, John J., ed. *The Heath Introduction to Fiction*, 5th ed. Lexington, Mass.: D. C. Heath, pp. 216–29.
[*Source: FP. Ten sections. 42.20, "in spite of you and Jennie!"*]

Hedges, Elaine R., ed. *The Yellow Wall-Paper*. Revised edition: A Complete and Accurate Rendition of the 1892 Edition, with a New Note on the Text. New York: The Feminist Press at the City University of New York, pp. 9–36.
[*Source: NE*]

Jacobus, Lee A., ed. *Literature: An Introduction to Critical Reading*. Upper Saddle River, N.J.: Prentice Hall, pp. 304–15.
[*Source: GR. Five sections.*]

Landy, Alice S., ed. *The Heath Introduction to Literature*, 5th ed. Lexington, Mass.: D. C. Heath, pp. 121–33.
[*Source: FP. Ten sections.*]

McMahon, Elizabeth, Susan X. Day, and Robert Funk, eds. *Literature and the Writing Process*, 4th ed. Upper Saddle River, N.J.: Prentice Hall, pp. 105–15.
[*Source: NE*]

Oates, Joyce Carol, ed. *American Gothic Tales*. New York: Plume, pp. 87–102.
[*Source: CW. 29.9, "expects that in man."*]

Wingard, Joel, ed. *Literature: Reading and Responding to Fiction, Poetry, Drama, and the Essay*. New York: HarperCollins, pp. 294–306.
[*Source: NE. Misdates NE as 1899.*]

1997

Barnet, Sylvan, Morton Berman, William Burto and William E. Cain, eds. *An Introduction to Literature*, 11th ed. New York: Longman, pp. 244–56.
[*Source: FP. Ten sections.*]

Barnet, Sylvan, Morton Berman, William Burto and William E. Cain, eds. *Literature: Thinking, Reading, and Writing Critically*, 2^d ed. New York: Longman, pp. 169–81.

[Source: FP. Ten sections.]

Gilbert, Sandra M., and Susan Gubar, eds. *The Norton Anthology of Literature by Women: The Tradition in English*, 2^d ed. New York: Norton, pp. 1133–44.

[Source: GR. Five sections. Misdates NE as May 1892.]

Guth, Hans P., and Gabriele L. Rico, eds. *Discovering Literature*, 2^d ed. Englewood Cliffs, N.J.: Prentice Hall, pp. 204–16.

[Source: NE. Beginning with the second section, the editors number the sections from I to XI.]

Henderson, Gloria Mason, Bill Day, and Sandra Stevenson Waller, eds. *Literature and Ourselves: A Thematic Introduction for Readers and Writers*, 2^d ed. New York: Longman, pp. 300–312.

[Source: GR. Six sections.]

Hunt, Douglas, ed. *The Riverside Anthology of Literature*, 3^d ed. Boston: Houghton, Mifflin, pp. 158–70.

[Source: GR. Six sections.]

Kirszner, Laurie G., and Stephen R. Mandell, eds. *Literature: Reading > Reacting > Writing*, 3^d ed. Fort Worth, Tex.: Harcourt Brace, pp. 160–72. [Compact 3^d ed., pp. 148–60.]

[Source: NE. The text is misdated 1899.]

McMichael, George, et al., eds. *Anthology of American Literature*, 6th ed. Upper Saddle River, N.J.: Prentice Hall, 2: 671–82.

[Source: NE. The editors preserve the variant spellings of "wall-paper."]

Pickering, James H., and Jeffrey D. Hoeper, eds. *Literature*, 5th ed. Upper Saddle River, N.J.: Prentice Hall, pp. 247–58.

[Source: NE]

Warner, J. Sterling, ed. *Thresholds: Literature-Based Composition*. New York: Harcourt Brace, pp. 389–401.

[Source: NE]

CPSIA information can be obtained at www.ICGtesting.com
Printed in the USA
LVOW042048040213

318585LV00001B/95/P